PHOENIX SOULED

PHOENIX SOULED

DRAGON OF SHADOW AND AIR BOOK TWELVE

JESS MOUNTIFIELD

DISRUPTIVE IMAGINATION®

THE PHOENIX SOULED TEAM

Thanks to our JIT Team:

Deb Mader
Dave Hicks
Dorothy Lloyd
Jeff Goode
Diane L. Smith

If We've missed anyone, please let us know!

Editor
SkyHunter Editing Team

LMBPN Publishing
PMB 196, 2540 South Maryland Pkwy
Las Vegas, NV 89109

Version 1.00 December 2021
eBook ISBN: 978-1-68500-053-0
Print ISBN: 978-1-68500-400-2

Dedication:

To Bryan. For being my Zephyr

CHAPTER ONE

For the first time in a while, I was excited. I was also nervous. Zephyr was too.

There was another dragon. After we thought Zephyr was the only one his entire life, this was huge. I was sitting with him as we waited for the plane to arrive. I and my mythicals were near the runway, having flown here to rendezvous with another group.

This dragon had met with the people who had been involved in opening the Texas portal, however. It was a worry, and we were supposed to be investigating the situation. We didn't want to put anyone else in danger.

Also, with the constant threat from Kirdash and his dark elves at the three open portals, none of us thought it was wise for anyone to come with us. I was worried about what might happen while we were away.

No one has attacked us for three days, and we're hopefully only going to be gone for one, Zephyr said.

It was a good point, but this whole thing bothered me. Neither of us was expecting another dragon. I could feel the mix of emotions Zephyr was keeping under control. This was a big deal for him as well.

I sent a wave of comfort toward him and leaned closer. His smooth scales were warm against my skin. In response, he wrapped his large tail around me. A dragon hug.

He spent most of his time in dragon form, especially when we had to fly, and leaning against the world's largest, most deadly predator and knowing he would do anything to protect me was reassuring.

Our moment didn't last any longer than that, however. Our ride arrived and let us know it was time to go. I wanted to turn around and go back to the Texas portal, but I also wanted to get on the plane and find out who this new dragon was.

As Zephyr morphed into human form, I stood up. The plane wasn't huge, but it was going to take us across the Atlantic to Ireland and the private farm that housed the most recently discovered portal. It made me wonder how many more were out there, but now wasn't the time to go looking for them.

We'd flown to the east coast, and it had been a gorgeous journey despite our hurry. We'd had brunch while we waited for our flight.

Do you think they'll have pizza? I asked Zephyr as we got on the plane.

If they have any sense, he replied, grinning and sitting next to me.

I panicked, remembering the last time we'd been on a plane. The military had been taking us from a base near LA to the Texas portal, which had been under attack. We'd also flown into battle on another occasion. They hadn't been relaxing flights.

However, we hoped this one would have a much happier resolution.

We chatted throughout the flight, talking about the places we wanted to visit when the world was safe once more. One day we wouldn't just talk about it. We would finally be done protecting the world, and all of us would be able to relax and not spend so much of our time fighting or training.

That didn't change the present, however. Zephyr's emotions flooded back when the green of land showed beneath us and the plane descended.

The farm was in the south of Ireland, surrounded by lush green fields and trees. The country was called the Emerald Isle for a reason, but seeing it was another matter. I fell in love with the place as we landed not far from the farm.

The US government had established contact and asked if we could pay a visit. All we knew was that we hadn't been refused. We weren't sure what to expect as a welcome, however.

The closer we got, the more agitated Zephyr became. He was rubbing one finger gently over the wristband on the other hand, tracing the stitching on the leather. I wished I could do more to help keep him calm. I took his hand and gave it a squeeze.

Not long after we landed, we got off, and Zephyr turned back into a dragon. I thanked our pilot, and we went the rest of the way alone. The plane was sticking around, and I hoped it would be a bigger party when we returned.

I gave Zephyr a nod before we powered into the air. I landed on his back, and Roth carried Sen to join us while Nuri flew ahead. We didn't have far to go, but we'd decided we wanted to arrive on our terms.

The sun was starting to set when we spotted the farm. Zephyr swooped lower. The portal was under a barn, but the front was open. We couldn't see it from our angle, but there were plenty of people going about the farm as if it were nothing unusual.

I worried that we'd come to the wrong place, but when we were spotted and no one freaked out, I relaxed. Someone called for the person in charge, and it wasn't long before he appeared. He came out of the house as we landed outside the front gate.

I stayed on Zephyr's back after he touched down so as to appear relaxed, then smiled and waved.

I can't see or feel their dragon, Zephyr informed me as I got down.

Feel? I asked.

Yeah. If he was nearby, I'd be able to feel him, and he'd be able to feel me.

Not sure how to respond to this information in front of a stranger, I exhaled and walked closer.

"Mr. Declan?" I asked.

"Depends who's asking, but, aye, you've found my farm. What is it you're wanting?"

"I'm hoping the US government told you we'd be stopping by," I said. "I believe we have something to chat about."

"They mentioned someone would be paying me a visit. Didn't mention anything about a dragon. I hope you mean to be civil."

"Entirely," I replied. His words hadn't been said with any fear. This farmer was confident he or the people with him could defend him. "I do want to talk to you about the portal to my homeworld in your barn. It would be nice to meet the dragon who has been coming through it if he's around."

The farmer blinked when I repeated what the US government had told him. I tried not to worry about it as he stepped back and opened the gate.

"Don't go breathing fire on anything or scaring the horses," Mr. Declan said as we stepped past him. I looked to see if anyone on the farm was not human.

"It's okay. Zephyr doesn't breathe fire. He's an air dragon, not a fire dragon."

The farmer lifted an eyebrow and glanced at Zephyr and me, then stalked off. I wasn't sure whether to be amused or irritated by his lack of knowledge. I'd gotten used to everyone knowing who I was, and it was strange to have to explain how safe we were.

Admittedly, if we were attacked, we would not be safe to be around. I had my helmet in my bag, along with all our other gear and more snacks than the average person consumed in a week.

We were led toward the barn that contained the portal, but the farmer stopped outside and didn't invite us in.

"The fella on the phone didn't say why you wanted to pay me a visit. Said he knew I had something interesting here and had made some friends. How do I know you're not going to do something unfriendly?"

"You don't," I replied. "But I don't mean any harm to anyone. I have spent the last few years of my life protecting elves and mythical creatures in the US and Mexico. There are plenty of videos of that on the internet, apparently."

"So, why are you here? No one is in danger here."

"I'm very glad to hear that. You are a good person, and I am sure you are doing a great job of helping those near you. I do want to talk to them about a threat on the other side of the portal and someone who visited the dragon here before us. We're struggling to keep the portals secure. You could say I'm here to ask for help."

The farmer studied me, and I tried to look normal. It was weird being studied to see if I was honest, but I tried not to flinch from his intense gaze.

"All right. You seem to know a fair bit, although I don't know how you know all that you do. But you might as well see it." The farmer finally backed up and let me see what was in the old barn.

I wasn't surprised to find the portal inside. There was a circle on the floor around it where there wasn't much in the way of the usual barn objects. There were stumps of rock where pillars must once have stood. They appeared to have been broken recently.

When I looked from them to the farmer, who had stopped near the portal, I caught him looking at me. He didn't say anything, however, or explain. I got the feeling he didn't much care what we thought or worked out, as if it wasn't his place to explain or divulge information.

Hoping the dragon wasn't far away, I went closer to the

portal. Much like the ones we had found previously, this was a large pool of shimmering light that hovered in the air. I imagine what it must have been like when they were safe and people traveled between them without hesitation.

I always approached them with dread, wondering what evil might lie on the other side. It was clear from the number of people near the barn who were going about their lives that no one here had the same trepidation. What was different about this portal?

Maybe it goes to a different place, Zephyr suggested.

Like, a different world? I asked as the farmer whistled for a young farmhand to come over.

I wasn't thinking that. Maybe a safe place on the other world. Another world is also possible.

"Go see if he's awake and let him know there are some visitors on this side. An elf, a dragon, a pegasus, a phoenix, and a dryad," the farmer said to the farmhand, flicking his head toward the portal.

I hid my surprise since he'd correctly identified my mythicals without me needing to name them. This was no ordinary farmer.

The farmhand didn't hesitate to go through the portal, walking into it as if he was going through a door.

"It's going to be a while," the farmer told us. "I've got work to do, but you're welcome to sit on a hay bale and wait or sit out in the yard. I'd appreciate you not going anywhere else, though."

"Of course. I'll wait in here with my mythicals. I know portal travel can seem slow to those on one end or the other and for those going through them."

"You've been through one?" the farmer asked, stopping.

"Yes. There's one in California that I went through several times to respond to a distress call from some elves. The dark elf was hunting them. We rescued them and a compound full of mythicals who had been locked up in cages. Some of them are still healing at a sanctuary in the US."

The farmer nodded. "That sounds dangerous and brave of you, yet you managed that and still seek help here?"

"Yeah. I might have pissed off the dark elf we stole them from," I replied, unable to keep from grinning.

There was a twinkle of amusement in the farmer's eyes, but it didn't last long. Someone called his name. He walked away, and I wondered what had led him to this point.

He did seem like a good man, but it was as if we'd stepped back in time two years and we were meeting mythicals and elves and humans who had no idea that the rest of the world knew they existed. Had they been that sheltered here? Or were they not interested? What could the humans and elves who had attacked the gate want here?

We could do nothing but wait for the dragon to come, and that was enough. It was another dragon, a type of mythical we had not expected to find, and we would hopefully meet them.

I sat near a hay bale and patted the ground beside me. Zephyr sighed and sat next to me.

You okay? I asked because I wanted to give him a chance to talk if he needed to while we had time.

I have a feeling this dragon doesn't like Earth much.

He might not have seen enough of it or met enough people

here to make an informed decision. Who knows? Maybe we can change his mind.

Zephyr leaned closer. Once again, we were waiting for someone, his tail around me and my body leaning against his. Sen came over and jumped onto my lap, picking up on Zephyr's unease. Nuri found a perch on a beam and tucked his head under his wing. Roth started munching on the hay.

With any luck, the dragon would be here soon.

CHAPTER TWO

Two hours later, I was losing my patience. How long did it take to find a dragon and get them to the portal to meet us?

However long it would take, it was too long. It had gotten dark, and the farmer had taken pity on us and brought us a couple of lanterns. Otherwise, we would have been sitting in the dark while we waited.

I got up and walked around for what must have been the tenth time. My butt was numb, and my legs had gone to sleep. If it hadn't been for the snacks I carried, I'd have also been hungry, as would Zephyr. I could easily carry supplies for Nuri and Sen, and Roth was surrounded by suitable food, but nothing here would satisfy a dragon.

I was starting to understand why the farmer had asked us not to scare his horses. I wondered why he hadn't asked us not to eat them.

Finally, the farmhand reappeared, pausing for a moment as he stepped into the dim light in the barn.

I moved toward him without thinking, and he jumped.

"The dragon will be here shortly. He isn't impressed, however."

"Well, that makes two of us," I replied.

The farmhand lifted his eyebrows at my tone. I didn't hide my disdain for how long we'd been kept waiting and folded my arms.

As much as I agree with that, we might want to play nice, Zephyr said as he stood up.

The farmhand looked at the large dragon and backed up.

"It's okay. He won't harm you. Not unless you hurt him or one of us."

Zephyr nodded to reassure the lad, but he appeared to decide that enough was enough, and he made his way to the door. I tried to hide my exasperation at being kept waiting for so long and instead look as if we'd been waiting for seconds.

Despite the farmhand's assurance that the dragon was on his way to join us, it was another twenty minutes before the portal rippled again, and someone stepped through. Here was another dragon in human form.

He looked us over and didn't seem impressed.

"Are you an elf?" he asked, his voice bright and brash, as if he were annoyed he had to ask. "Or a dragon in human form?"

"Elf," I replied. "We thought Zephyr was the only dragon left."

The other dragon didn't respond, just glanced at Zephyr, then folded his arms across his chest.

"Let me guess. You've come here to demand I shut the portal and stop what I'm doing? I'll save you the trouble. I don't answer to you or your lineage, and I won't be stopping anything."

"Oh, no. We weren't here to ask you to stop anything," I said, taking a step forward. "We're truly excited about meeting another dragon. Zephyr thought he was alone, and..."

My voice trailed off as I realized Zephyr and this guy were staring at each other, the tension mounting. I felt as if I'd missed something, and I had no idea what it was.

He's a gold dragon, Zephyr commented.

And you're a brass one. Does it matter? Please tell me that the elven world didn't assign a hierarchy or value to the color of your scales?

No, not as such. The great dragon that flew with Tuviel was brass, and there was a gold dragon who opposed a lot of their decisions. Wanted to handle the dark lord another way. There was merit to some of the ideas, but they often got elves killed.

Oh. And he is holding a grudge because of the color of your scales?

Something like that.

"I don't know if it helps, but we wanted to check that you were okay here and find out if you were aware of how active the dark elf is. Especially since some of the dark elf's pawns came here weeks ago," I said to bring the dragon's attention back to me.

"I'm fine here, and I didn't deal with them. I don't particularly want to deal with you. If that's truly all you wanted, you can go back to whatever rock you have been hiding under for the last little while and stay there."

The dragon turned to go, but Zephyr growled and lifted more.

"Do you have nothing else to say?" Zephyr asked. "Do you know what Kirdash will do if he finds you?"

"He won't find me, runt," the guy replied, squaring up with Zephyr despite being in a different form. "I know how to hide from him and protect everyone with me. I wouldn't expect Tuviel's heir and her pet to understand that."

"I'm not Tuviel's heir," I replied. "Not exactly."

That made the dragon pause, and he looked at me, his eyebrow raised.

"I was made in a lab by an elf who was sick of the portals being closed and wanted to be reunited with the mythicals we've been shut off from. He spliced my DNA with that of a load of different elves and a dragon."

"That's...not what I expected." The dragon stepped closer, then reached out and grabbed my chin. I blinked as he tilted my head to the side and studied me in the light of the lantern.

Zephyr growled and came closer, his tail swishing across the floor.

I put my hand out to the side to let my dragon know that I was okay before the two of them came to blows, but the one looking me over didn't react to the aggressive response.

"You do have more in you than a glance suggested. You're still a mutt of all the elves who abandoned us."

"Well, they weren't going to have anyone else's DNA to work with, were they?" I pointed out without thinking. "No one else was here."

The dragon's mouth twitched as he let go of me.

"So, what do they call you, elf?"

"Henera, mostly. I go by Aella normally. That's what my mother called me."

"Henera?" He chuckled, but it was not an indication of amusement. It was disdain.

"Yeah. I wasn't amused at first either. I have four elements and four bonds." I pointed at each mythical and gently used each element that matched in some small way to make my point. "After that, it stuck."

The dragon looked at everyone and then back at me. "I'll ask one last time. Why are you here?"

"Truly, we're here to see if you need our aid and if you were aware that Kirdash was a threat. I think we assumed you were refugees like the ones we rescued through another portal last week."

"I'm not. Your dragon could have told you that. His genetic memories would let him know my ancestors found a haven. Somewhere dragons could get to."

"They did," Zephyr replied, relaxing now that he knew I wasn't in any danger. "But I'm the last of my line. I had no way of knowing if yours had survived."

There was another change in the demeanor of the dragon, and he backed up.

"Well, you've learned what you needed to. I'm safe. So are the few mythicals under my care. I'm not interested in anything else. Your predecessors closed the portals on us a long time ago, and we've had to rely on ourselves. If you can't handle anything this dark elf throws at you, that's your problem."

Zephyr growled, and I could feel waves of mixed emotions coming off him.

I think we need to let this one go, I told him. *This dragon wants to be left alone. I'm sorry.*

"I'm glad you're safe," I continued aloud. "And for what it's worth, I'm truly sorry you and everyone else on the other side got shut off from this world and the mythicals on it. I have no idea what that was like, but it can't have been easy."

"You know nothing of what it was like," the dragon said, stepping back into the portal.

Sighing, I tried not to let all my disappointment show and sent comfort to Zephyr. This hadn't been what I'd hoped for, and I couldn't imagine how much worse it was for him.

He'd thought he was the last of his kind. Then he found out that the only other dragon he knew about didn't want anything to do with him and was holding a millennia-old grudge against his type of dragon.

It was unfair, and it made me worry about the portals and how we were going to face Kirdash. Of all the responses I'd expected from the dragon, indifference hadn't been one of them.

I ran my hand over Zephyr's scales as we walked out of the barn and made our way to the gate. When we reached it, I realized how tired I was, and I covered a yawn. The excitement, the flying, and then the long wait had worn me out. On top of that, I'd learned something I probably ought to have known.

Did you remember there were dragons who had hidden over there? I asked Zephyr.

Yes and no. The memories are there, but the events happened long ago. Until recently, I considered everyone on the other side of the portals cut off from us. I didn't think about what one lineage of dragons might have been doing, given that so much time had passed.

I exhaled, knowing that it was wrong of me to be irritable with Zephyr over the exchange. It wasn't his fault that the dragon had a grudge against our ancestors as much as it wasn't mine.

When we got to the gate, the farmer stepped out of a small building nearby.

"You finished talking to Nerik?" the man asked.

"Yes," I replied, not hiding my annoyance. "He doesn't seem to like others much."

"He does what he thinks is best, like most." The farmer looked me over as he spoke.

Relaxing, I nodded. He was right, even if I didn't like it. Roth nuzzled my hand when I paused, and Zephyr lowered his head and leaned close.

"You look like you're tired and hungry. The missus is no doubt finishing up dinner as we speak. There's always extra. Why don't you all come in and eat? I can't feed the dragon in dragon form, though."

Zephyr morphed into human form.

"Thank you," he said sadly.

We followed the farmer to the house. We'd come all this way, and we might as well have a good meal before we flew back, even if it wasn't likely to be pizza.

Inside were more people than I'd expected, farmhands as well as several women. I smiled at whoever glanced my way, but they were all focused on getting dishes on the table, everyone knowing their place and helping get the enormous amount of food from kitchen to table.

Without anyone saying anything, several chairs were

added, and a large bowl was placed on a stool near Roth. There was a saucer of water supplied between the two new chairs for Sen and a bird perch with a bowl for Nuri. It was clear that everyone here was used to feeding animals or mythicals.

"Sit and dig in. You look half-famished," Mrs. Declan said when the food was on the table and everyone had pulled out chairs to sit.

I nodded and did as she suggested, grateful when she sat next to me. As she offered me some slices of bread, I realized this was the first time I'd been in a room full of strangers since I met Minsheng.

I felt like that frightened girl in the Chinese restaurant Minsheng ran, being offered food and not sure if I should accept it or if I was safe.

We're safe. They're protective about the portal and any myth-icals. There's elf blood in them.

I sighed. Zephyr's words and emotions calmed me, but I couldn't help but think of the dragon and his confidence that he was hidden from Kirdash. Did he not realize that there was no hiding from someone like the dark elf? Kirdash would find him if he learned he was there.

Over the course of the next hour, I relaxed, telling Allison, the farmer's wife, about my journey and my life so far. She told me about the farm and that they'd had the open portal in the barn for as long as she could remember, and that for years, the dragon had traded magic and items from the other side for food.

It made me wonder who had opened the portal and when, but Allison assured me it had been open her whole life and not a new discovery even then. Whoever had opened it, they weren't likely to be a threat. It was a comfort to take that back to the US with me, even if I was returning empty-handed.

I was getting up from dinner, thanking the farmer and his wife profusely for their kindness, especially when she wrapped us up a generous portion of leftovers for the flight home, when I heard footsteps outside. One of the farmhands went to see who it was, but I didn't get a chance to follow since Allison put her hand on my shoulder.

"Come back in a few weeks if you can," she said. "The dragon sometimes takes a while to accept new faces. He comes through on Mondays without fail."

I nodded, grateful for the invitation, although the farmer raised his eyebrows at his wife's offer. I had a feeling this wasn't something they normally told visitors.

"Soldiers want the girl and her pets," the farmhand said as he came back in.

"We're not pets," Zephyr replied with the same level of irritation the other dragon had shown earlier.

I stifled a smile at his demeanor despite agreeing with him.

"They're bonded mythicals. It's like being a soulmate," I added in a gentle tone, turning my mind to what the kid had said.

"What did the soldiers want?" Zephyr asked, sounding normal again.

"Didn't say. Said to hurry."

There was no doubt in my mind what could make them want to hurry us. The dark elf must have attacked through the portal. That might mean everyone we cared about was in danger.

CHAPTER THREE

Every minute that ticked by was agony. The soldiers confirmed that all three portals were under attack, and they would fly us back to the US as swiftly as they could. By the time we arrived, the battle might be over, or a portal might have been lost.

The latter wasn't a comforting thought. I hoped the elves and the soldiers worked well together in my absence.

Sen, Roth, and Nuri were asleep in the back of the plane. The three of them were always able to sleep, no matter what was coming, but Zephyr and I were awake.

We'd talked about our meeting with the dragon twice, and I was more impressed with how polite Zephyr had been each time. It sounded as if the mythical was holding one massive grudge, and I wasn't sure how I felt about it.

I could understand it must have felt awful to be trapped on the other side of the portals with the dark elf. I was also aware that the greats had thought they had contained the dark elf in a prison. He was supposed to be harmless.

If they'd been confident he would stay confined, they would not have shut the portals and blocked them. They knew they were abandoning the other mythicals. Many knew it was coming. Most were given a choice of planet.

I leaned against Zephyr, who was in human form and had his arm around me. It was a point he hadn't brought up before, and it made me realize how much he knew from his memories that I would have to learn. I was starting to understand why the dragons were considered wise. They had a big advantage.

Of course, none of this impacted the emotions I was feeling or the fear about what was happening at the portals. No matter how awesome our teams were and how good a plan there was, Kirdash was driven and angry, and our people were used to me leading them into battle.

Unable to sit still any longer and sure we must have been in the air long enough to be close to the Texas site, I got up. Zephyr met my gaze but didn't join me, choosing to stay where he was and keep an eye on our sleeping mythicals.

I made my way to the cockpit and the pilot and tried to work out where we were from the terrain. It was a useless endeavor since it was dark, and I was never very good at that anyway.

This was going to get worse as we got closer, and the pilot was doing his best, judging by the concentration on his face as he flew. I was about to turn and leave him be when he saw me standing there.

"Another twenty minutes, and you should be good to launch out the back and get there quicker than we can position and land," the pilot informed me.

"Thank you," I replied, choosing not to voice my frustration with not being there sooner.

Now wasn't the time to make anyone feel bad for doing their best, no matter how impatient I was. Not sure what else to do while I waited, however, I went back to the main cabin of the plane, pulled my helmet out of my pack, and put it on.

I got out Sen's armor, Roth's head pack to focus his water blasts, and the gloves that helped me direct my air jets. That left Zephyr's vine-whip dagger, but he carried that at all times. It morphed with him, being tied to one of his horns in dragon form and through a loop of his belt when in human form.

I didn't pretend to understand how his transformation worked and where his clothes all came from, but I was glad it did, and he could shift from one form to the other so easily.

It's all an illusion, Zephyr said, obviously listening to my thoughts. *It's also a rearrangement of everything that's there.*

You don't know how it works either, do you?

Nope. I can pretend to, though, right?

To everyone else.

It's not as if I can hide anything from you. You're inside my head.

I grinned as I made my way back to him and the rest of our bonded mythicals. Sen was beginning to stir, probably disturbed by the noise. Trying not to worry about how late we might be to the battle, I helped her don the dragon scale armor and then pulled on my gloves.

Zephyr put the headband on Roth, helping the water horse get it into place and making sure it would stay there.

Nuri flew over and landed on my shoulder, and the team was ready for whatever we were going to walk into. I hoped it wasn't for nothing.

There was still time to wait, but the co-pilot went to the back hatch. We'd not originally been planning to jump out of it, but if the battle still raged, it was the fastest way to join it. We hadn't heard anything in the last hour about the base being safe or dark.

The last part had me worried. That no one was responding didn't bode well. Although the soldiers on the plane had assured me they frequently lost contact when magic was thrown around the site, it hadn't occurred to me that there were people other than the President who checked on us.

As soon as the back of the plane opened, I heard the engines and could reach out with my mind toward the ground with more ease. We were still some distance from the Texas portal, but I hoped I would be able to hear or feel a battle or the elves' repair work or anything that would make it obvious they were still alive.

Instead, there was nothing but the noise of the engine. I put aside my fears and focused on getting ready to jump out of the plane.

With Sen tucked into my jacket, I moved to the open hatch. I wasn't sure it was time to jump, but I'd had enough of the waiting and not knowing what was happening. We were about to find out.

"Find somewhere safe to land nearby and try to stay out of trouble," I said to a soldier near me and nodded to Zephyr.

Without another word, we powered out the back hatch

and moved toward the portal. In the dark, I couldn't see where the rest of my mythicals were since we had spread out as we left the plane. Thankfully, our bond meant I could feel the location of each of them.

As the one able to see best in the dark, Zephyr led the way, and we followed. I explored the air around us, letting Zephyr point me toward the target.

There were lights ahead, but it took a while to make out the portal base. It didn't look like it had when we'd left. The cavern was open on top again.

Panic rose inside me and I felt for people next, not sure anyone was still alive. Fortunately, I could feel movements in the air as people shifted. There were lots outside the main building and in hastily erected shelters, thrown together by earth elves in a hurry.

I think they've lost control of the portal, Zephyr said. *Only thing that makes sense.*

And they're still fighting?

Sort of. Maybe a stalemate now.

Our folks might know we're due here soon.

Or be hoping for it.

I wasn't about to argue with him. It was clear we were needed, and I would always go where I could make a difference, especially to fight the dark elf and his forces.

By the time we could see a force in a circle around the main building and the cavern, I was sure Zephyr was right. The soldiers and mythicals stationed here had lost control of the portal, and dark elves were pushing out and beyond.

I wondered why the dark elves weren't flying out of the hole in the cavern, but no sooner had I thought that than an air elf did just that. A bullet came from their right and hit the dark elf. They died, and their lifeless body fell back into the portal room.

I wanted to be sure I wouldn't get hurt if I flew in, but I hadn't seen which direction the bullet had come from, so I hung back to find someone.

Eventually, I spotted Minsheng, my Shishou, helping someone injured. I landed beside him and saw relief wash over his face when he realized who I was.

"We were attacked. Couldn't hold it without you," he said, the words tumbling out. He was focused on the person before him.

"I heard. I'm here now. What are we up against, and who can still fight?"

"All the soldiers still have ammo, but most elves are drained. We got cut off from supplies, and the food wasn't due to be restocked until tomorrow, so there's not a lot to hand out."

I put a hand on Minsheng's shoulder as he continued to brief me.

We're going to have to wade in, push this lot back, and hope they rally around us, Zephyr said.

I didn't doubt that he was correct. We were going to have to throw what we had at it and hope for the best. If nothing else, it would give everyone who noticed us hope and bring them back into the fight.

I walked toward one of the hastily erected defenses and the soldiers waiting there. Relief rushed through me when I saw the major.

He spotted me and sagged.

"Henera," he whispered. "I wish you'd arrived sooner."

Although I wasn't sure I had time for his indecision, I tried not to fret as I crouched beside him.

"Tell me briefly what's happened so far. We'll see if we can change the tide."

The major took a deep breath, looked at the soldier beside him, and nodded.

"The dark elf sent another wave of foot soldiers. We held them back to begin with. The elves did their best and used strategies from the previous battles to force them back, but there were too many of them, and we didn't have the capacity to keep the pressure up."

"So, it drained the elves?" I asked.

"I think so. We had to fall back. One of them held an air barrier for a long time. Made sure we were all past her and in a safe place before she let go. Collapsed from over-extending. I tried to grab her and haul her into my team, but the dark elves got to her first."

I exhaled, sure he'd told me that the dark elves had killed one of the precious few air elves we had. I pictured the Amcika elf who had been one of the first to defect after I had been trapped there and had to fight my way out. I hoped I was wrong and she was still alive, but if that was true, it meant someone else was dead.

"How far out has the enemy spread? Have any gotten into the wilderness around here?"

"I don't believe so, but I can't say for sure. It's dark and chaotic, and some have tried, but there's plenty of other stuff going on.

"Are any reinforcements due to arrive?" I hoped the answer was yes and soon, but I couldn't wait. There wouldn't be any elves to fight, even if I did gain more scared soldiers.

"Yes. The President is flying in more troops, but they've got a long way to come, and I don't know when they'll get here."

That told me what I needed to know. I had to attack now, especially if the dark elf continued to send troops through the portal. I had to wear them out and send them back.

Reaching for the crystals in the helmet I wore, I decided it was time to get the attack underway. I didn't move, however. I needed something to hold back the attacks as well as drive the dark elves back, and I thought about the freezing barriers Simon had taught me how to make.

I started with those, staying under cover as Zephyr merged his control with mine and a nearby water elf helped Roth suck liquid out of a large tub that was normally in the barracks. I didn't make as huge a barrier as I wanted since we had to fire around it and move it through the building, but it was large enough to keep my mythicals and me safe.

It took a while to pull the heat out of it, something that wasn't easy to do and maintain in Texas. I did my best, however, then stood up.

Still not able to see well, I used my abilities to feel for the air and find out who was where. Now and then, I butted against a mind in control, but I pushed past them all, boosted by everything I was wearing and could access. It was time for the dark elf army to see if they could fight me and live.

CHAPTER FOUR

The dark elves didn't know what hit them. It was clear that many of them were low on power and hadn't been able to rest much, pushed by the soldiers on the base even if they weren't by the other elves. I was fresh, however.

On the plane on the way here, I'd added power to my helmet, knowing it would regenerate as I was flown closer. I used it to power all my attacks.

I helped Roth direct a blast of water into two dark elves. It washed them into the path of some soldiers, who shot them before they'd had a chance to recover. Not sure what to do, the soldiers left them there, either dead or injured, and followed me deeper into the site.

Moving on and taking out dark elves, I made my way toward the main building.

When I reached allies who had been stranded or hurt, a lot of them fell in with me, taking advantage of my air barrier and the protection to regroup. Before long, I needed to make it wider, but I didn't stop or slow my advance.

I wasn't far from the main building when someone challenged my mind. I realized I had pushed into someone else and the air they wanted to retain control of. Unlike my fights to get here, this dark elf had energy left, and they were prepared to use it. I felt the heat as they made a fireball.

I took the element away from them and did the opposite: made it cold. A moment later, I used a blast of air to pin them to the floor, and Sen hit them with darts.

Zephyr challenged a powerful earth elf who was trying to pull down or alter the main building. My dragon took control and wrapped a vine-whip dagger plant around the dark elf so tight they couldn't move a limb. They couldn't talk, the vine having gagged them as well.

I smiled about this battle being easy so far, but the smugness didn't last long. Up ahead, I spotted one of the robed dark elves who had been inside the Mexican mountain. So far, we had encountered none of the armored dark elves from the last battle, but at least one had come with her.

Although the fire elf twin had perished, the female water twin who had been with him had managed to get back to the portal before I could stop her. Our eyes locked, but before either of us could do anything, Roth hit her with a blast of water.

It would have been funny if it hadn't rebounded off her and hit the armored dark elf beside her. The elemental magic would power his armor, so it was going to make the fight harder.

Where's the armor we collected the last time? Zephyr asked me, but I shrugged in response. It was supposed to be on the base somewhere, but I'd not seen anyone wearing it, and I wasn't sure who had the use allocated to them. Some of our elves weren't here.

Trying not to think about them or what might be happening elsewhere, I used earth to pull the ground out from beneath the two dark elves. I then took control of the water around them. I wasn't sure what element the armored elf was, but so far, he wasn't hitting me with anything else.

Before they could get to their feet, Sen and Nuri came hurtling in. Sen blasted ice bolts at the water elf, and Nuri burst into flame in front of the armored elf. It provided another distraction and allowed Zephyr and me to sprint across the distance. I grabbed the water elf's wrist and spun her around before slamming her to the ground.

Within seconds, a nearby soldier and Sen had struck her with enough darts to take her out. Zephyr had a grip on the other elf, but the pain was growing in my hand. The armor was defending the dark elf, and I could feel the agony it was causing Zephyr through our bond.

I roundhouse-kicked the guy, toppling him, then Zephyr swept his legs. With the dragon pinning him, Sen and I quickly unbuckled his armor and yanked it off.

As soon as it was off, the tingle of the magic it harnessed deactivated. I used air to hold the elf, and Zephyr held the armor out to me.

It's far too big for me, I replied, although I wished to accept it.

Zephyr looked as if he were going to argue, but the dark elf chose that moment to lash out with a small blade he had hidden somewhere. The dagger plant whipped out a branch and sent the shining blade flying.

I hit the dark elf with air again, and Sen shot him with her dart gun. Within seconds, he was out for the count too.

I waited for Zephyr to put the armor on. No one else was paying us any attention; all the elves around us were locked in battle. I looked for another dark elf wearing armor. There had to be a smaller set on a female somewhere. I would find it.

Nothing caught my eye. I headed toward the main building. Some dark elves were in our way, barricaded outside.

Aware that we needed to act before many more elves could come through the portal, I kept walking, hurling elements and keeping the barrier up in front of us as I did.

Several fireballs struck the barrier a moment later. It hissed and steamed when their heat hit cold and reacted. It would have been beautiful if it hadn't been deadly and aimed at me.

Focused on repairing the damage to the barrier where it heated up, I let Zephyr and the others take the offensive. I was feeling the drain on my powers and we weren't inside yet, so I started pulling from the air crystal in my helmet.

I was sure that there were more of our elves somewhere. There weren't many out here, and I could hear the flames crackling and feel the occasional shake of the earth. With any luck, they were inside, and I could reinforce a position.

When I reached another earth elemental, he challenged me for control of the ground beneath his feet. I punched him in the face, using the air elemental crystal to speed up and add extra force to the hit. He went down, unconscious and unmoving. The soldiers behind me finished him off with darts.

We formed a wedge toward the door, then I was hit from the side by an air blast. It almost knocked me off my feet, but I used the air to cushion, then right myself as if I'd bounced on a trampoline. Finding the elf who had hit me, I grabbed control of the air around her and blasted her back.

This feels too easy, Zephyr said as he used vines to turn three dark elves upside-down. The soldiers took them out while they were still adjusting to being the wrong way up.

They have been fighting a long time, I pointed out, but I could see what Zephyr meant. There was no organization. In previous battles, the dark elves teamed up with other elementals of the same type and merged their control. This time, we had been able to pick off all these elves because they were on their own.

Roth trampled an elf who had been hiding in an earth bunker after filling it with water and forcing him to climb out. I realized we'd cleared the path to the door.

Wondering if it was a trap, I widened my air barrier and encouraged Sen and Zephyr to join me behind it. The doors to the base were wide open, but it was dimly lit inside. The emergency lighting was on, shedding a strange red glow on everything. It was a creepy color and I slowed, taking seconds to process what I saw.

I now had an explanation for why the elves outside weren't in teams. The corridors were lined with dead dark elves. Many of them had been shot, but from the smell and the way they looked, they'd been electrocuted.

Glancing at Zephyr, I stepped tentatively, moving the

water on the floor away from our feet in case it carried a live current. His mind was merged with mine and made the task easier, but I wasn't sure if it was necessary.

Ahead and to the left, I saw some living dark elves behind a large door that had been ripped off its hinges. They were trading elemental blasts with someone inside a nearby room.

Sure that meant allies in need of rescuing, I hurried down the hallway and seized control of everything outside the room. That drew the attention of the dark elves, three of them reeling as I stole their elements.

Before any of them could react, I hit them with the door they were holding. One of them fell over and was electrocuted, answering my question.

"Stay out of the water. It's live," I yelled to the people behind me. I used air to sweep Sen over the water and bring her onto my shoulder. Roth hesitated; I had helped him so far, but he was made of water.

Go back outside, I told the water pegasus, terrified of what the water would do to him if he stepped in it without me keeping it away from all of us.

Thankfully he didn't argue, and he could help out there. With that taken care of, I advanced on the two dark elves ahead. They were wary since Zephyr and I were in control of the elements around them.

We'd almost reached the entrance to the room when someone jetted out fire and singed the door I'd blasted. I tried not to let my focus slip. There might be fewer enemies, and they might look as if they were out of energy, but I'd been lured in by that stratagem before.

Of course, this time, I wasn't alone. There were soldiers

with me, and there were more mythicals in the building, too.

We kept pushing the dark elves back, using a steady air blast to get them to retreat until we reached the room they'd been attacking. In the gloomy interior, two elves and the general were standing on a desk whose legs were in the water. Seth smiled at me.

"Told you we were about to be rescued," Seth said to the general.

The older officer didn't look convinced that this was good news, but he nodded in my direction.

"Any idea where Emily is?" I asked, thinking about how quickly she'd probably get the water out of the way and clear the building.

"I think she's wherever this electrified water came from. It saved our bacon...sort of." Seth looked around as if he weren't sure the water was a good idea anymore.

I considered moving it, but I suspected having it on the ground was helping more than hindering us. I couldn't leave the others where they were, however. If more dark elves came along, they would be easy targets. Despite Seth's bravado, I had saved them.

I took control of the water and parted it, making sure the floor was dry in a path toward the doorway. The three of them rushed over.

The major had found some wooden planks from somewhere and was laying them through the water behind me. It wasn't a perfect solution, and I had to continue to dry a path to the end of each plank before they got clear, but they had a way out that didn't further tax my abilities.

Grateful I wasn't doing this alone, I moved down the

hall toward the portal room. The doors along the route opened to the boardroom and the office the general usually used, both empty.

Not wanting to waste more time or risk being surprised by more dark elves when Zephyr and I were holding back the electrified water, we continued to the cavern.

A strange glow filled the room, and sparks crackled here and there. Moonlight shone through the open ceiling. I stopped and took in the scene.

A group of dark elves was gathered around the portal. They were standing in the dry section of the room, and a couple of powerful water elves in the middle were holding back the deadly flood. More elves came through, forcing the water elves to widen the area.

It appeared like they were straining to cope.

Emily is at the back. With Simon.

I looked where Zephyr pointed, seeing the pair in the gloom. They were sitting on a ledge partway up the cavern wall, safe and dry. Simon had an air barrier up. Emily sat behind it with him. She was staring at the water elves with a look of intense concentration on her face.

The attackers were trapped. Simon held the newcomers off while Emily battled the dark elves controlling the water. The dark elves, in turn, protected their company, allowing them to attack Simon and Emily.

We had walked in on a stalemate, but I could tell it wouldn't stay that way for long. As more dark elves came through the portal, the pressure would increase until Emily or Simon gave.

I combined my control and power with Emily's and

Simon's, merging it with Zephyr's. They noticed I was there, the task having consumed their attention.

I gave them a nod of support, lending them my power as I stood in the doorway to the hall. I wasn't going to let them struggle anymore.

Simon grew the barrier, taking the heat off him and Emily enough that the dark elves noticed.

Some of them turned my way, but the first fireball that came toward me instead of them merely hit the barrier I had in place.

Emily locked eyes with one of the water elves and reached out, both holding her ground and challenging the dark elf. Although part of me wanted to smash their minds to get the fight over and done with, there was merit in holding back. Emily needed to show her strength and control.

I gave her a boost from the water crystal in my helmet, and within seconds, she wrested control from the water elves, making them stagger. They recovered quickly, but Emily let the water go, and it did as expected: crashed across the floor and surrounded the dark elves.

They started writhing, and those who could hurled themselves back through the portal. It wasn't an ideal way to end a fight, and Emily got a strange look on her face when she realized she'd killed several dark elves. I knew that expression. It appeared when a person realized they had killed someone who was trying to kill them and hadn't hesitated.

Giving her time to process, I looked for the source of the electricity. The portal was clear, and it was time to reclaim the area.

CHAPTER FIVE

Trying not to cry in front of the others but not sure how else to react, I helped several of the earth elves dig graves. The battle was over and we'd mostly won, but as we created final resting places, it was hard to feel like we had. We'd lost three elves in the battle, along with a centaur and four soldiers.

Although the soldiers' bodies had been returned to their families, the centaur and the elves would be entombed where they fell. The Sanctuary had limited space, and the Texas portal site had become home for the elves defending it.

I helped lower the bodies into the graves, pausing once all four were in place. Simon had agreed to say a few words about their sacrifice. I thought back to how I'd found him the night before. He'd been using his last scraps of elemental power to keep Emily alive and the dark elves from overrunning the base, willing to sacrifice himself if necessary.

Simon had once killed one of my friends, and I occasionally remembered that when the elf was in battle. Simon had also created me, in conjunction with a host of others: gnomes, dwarves, and the genetic material of more great mythicals than anyone deserved to be descended from. I still didn't know how I felt about him, but I could respect his willingness to give everything to defend this planet we all called home.

Now that the majority of my job was done, I stepped back into the crowd. Most people on the base had gathered to honor our fallen, and there weren't many dry eyes. It made me feel better for struggling to hold back my own tears. I had not known any of the dead very well, but I had fought with them.

I should never have left the portal site to go to Ireland. It was a long way for me to go with my mythicals when the portals were less protected, and someone else could have gone and been told the dragon wasn't interested in us.

There was a good chance that anyone else who had gone would have had a better chance than the direct descendants of the very mythicals the new dragon held a family grudge against. At the least, they probably wouldn't have done any worse than we had.

We shouldn't blame ourselves, Zephyr told me. *We didn't attack our friends.*

But we weren't there to save them, either.

We can't be. Not all the time. No one can. It wasn't our fault. The dark elves attacked the base, and mythicals died. Kirdash spreads destruction and death wherever he goes. He always has.

It sounds as if you remember him, I said over the background noise of the dead being honored and those who wanted to add a handful of dirt to each grave.

Although I was sure it was my fault, Zephyr had a point. I couldn't be rigid. I had to accept that I was saving people from an enemy who was more powerful than I was. Fighting them was a dance of wills each time.

I remember many things about him. I don't remember meeting him face to face, but I know how he thinks and what happens to those who don't obey him. There's also talk about something that can be done by him and him alone. A way he uses his magic that is not how it was intended.

Tell me about it. He also has all four elements, but it doesn't feel like the way I have them. It feels as if they were somehow added on, and that shouldn't have been possible.

And he can manipulate mythical bonds.

I had forgotten he was capable of doing that. More than once, when his mind had connected to ours through the portal, he had attacked our bonds, and it had felt as if he were going to break them.

No part of me wanted to repeat how it had felt, but we'd talked at length about what he might be capable of. He didn't appear to have any bonded mythicals of his own. It would have been strange, but I'd noticed that there were mythicals in prisons and capture centers all over his world. I'd rescued all the mythicals from one and considered doing more, but for now, Kirdash was the only one who knew what he could do with bonded mythicals.

As soon as the funeral was over and I'd done my part, I made my way to the portal room. I wanted some time alone and that the base was safe while I got it.

Not for the first time, I considered walking through it and finding out what was on the other side of this one, but if I'd been given the right information, this one led to a room inside the heart of Kirdash's palace. I wasn't sure about that part, but there wasn't much I could do to check. Instead, I reached toward it with my mind.

The first few times I had reached through the barely open portal, there had been a female elf. She'd told me she was a slave in the palace and about the other portal and the refugees. I had rescued everyone she'd told me to, and it had led to where I was now, with another open portal and the danger of Kirdash showing up at any moment.

When I'd realized that the elves who had attacked the base and destroyed the pillars had been hiding among the refugees, I was sure it had been a ruse and the elf I'd talked to didn't exist—or if she did, she had used me to open another portal and bring those elves here.

There was no way to be sure. The young female elf hadn't appeared since.

I took another step toward the portal, and Zephyr's arm snaked around me.

Be careful, he said, thankfully not telling me not to attempt anything. He knew me, so he understood that I needed to get some idea of what was on the other side. I wanted to know if we had been betrayed and if there were slaves.

Some of the refugees might have answers, but they had harbored the elves who had betrayed us. Even if they'd not done it deliberately, someone had set up my defeat and been the mastermind behind it all.

My mind touched the edge of the portal and was pulled in, the grip strange and disorienting at first. I had no idea if others could allow their minds to be transported while their bodies were left behind, but I wasn't going to encourage it. It was a huge drain on the energy of the elf who acted in this manner.

Every time I had considered suggesting others try to communicate and gather intel for us, I thought about the danger. I didn't want anyone else to take the risk, which meant I had to do it.

After several long, agonizing minutes, my mind popped out on the other end. I focused on the elements. The magical part of my mind had moved across, the part of me that could control elements, which meant I couldn't see in the conventional sense.

I could take control of the air over there, and the fire, water, and earth. Between the four, I could make up a picture of what I saw. It was a skill that had taken me a while to master, but I quickly put it to good use. Reaching out, I connected in a circle around the portal.

It was inside a room, as I'd been led to believe, and I could feel the mark of Kirdash on all the elements around it. This was a place where he spent a lot of time.

My reach on the other side was limited, but I worked out that it was inside a building and guarded, but not in an aggressive way. Elves hurried past, and it seemed to be in the center of a large, symmetrical building.

Whatever it was housed in, this was an important portal.

As I grew tired and it became more difficult to feel the elements on the other side, I pulled my mind back. There was only so much something like this could tell us about what we should expect from the forces Kirdash had prepared.

When my mind returned to my body, I found Minsheng

and the general nearby. I tried not to look startled or show my emotions and tiredness, but I couldn't muster a smile either.

"We should have a chat," the general began. "The President would like to hear how we're all faring, and I'm sure that we could do with a moment to reflect on possible new strategies."

I wasn't sure if this was a reprimand when it was the general who had asked me to go visit a dragon, but it was best to attend the meeting and see what could be done. We weren't going to stop Kirdash if we didn't work together.

With a heavy heart, I went to the office with the general and Minsheng. My mythicals came too, although some of them would find the meetings difficult. We'd agreed a long time ago that we were equals when it came to making decisions about our future. As much as possible, anyway.

The President was on a video call and waiting for us, but I was surprised to see that Cherisse, Sierrathen, and Vestan were there as well. The elves were at the other major locations: Cherisse in Mexico at the first portal, Sierrathen in California at the portal I'd opened, and Vestan at the Sanctuary.

It was an important meeting.

For the first ten minutes, we talked about how our sites had fared in terms of attacks. The Sanctuary had been safe, but Vestan reported that another orb was missing. That was a worry, given the lack of need for them now that the Sanctuary wasn't hidden and welcomed visitors.

I was dismayed to hear that the other portals had been pushed hard and the earth elves had been momentarily overwhelmed at the other sites despite the dark elf attacking through the Texas portal as well. It seemed he had the forces to push us hard at three sites at once, and we would be hard-pressed to stop him.

It was a terrifying thought, and that was why everyone was on this call together. I didn't doubt that they wanted to do something about it, and it wasn't necessarily going to be something I thought was wise.

"We need to find a way to close these portals," the President said when everyone had finished making their reports and confirming my fears.

"I agree," Sierrathen said a fraction of a second before Vestan.

I expected Cherisse to be angry, but she just sighed.

"We need to close some of them if nothing else. We do not have the strength to hold this many that are so spread out."

Everyone looked at me for my response.

I didn't want to close the portals. There was merit in it, but it hadn't worked for the old-time elves. It had merely delayed the problem and subjected the mythicals on the other planet to a millennium of slavery and difficulty. If I was the Henera and could do anything to atone for the actions of my ancestors, closing the portals wasn't an option.

But I could see the hope in their eyes.

"Is it possible?" I asked to buy time.

"It was before," the President replied.

"There are books on the matter," Vestan added. "Our libraries and resources aren't in the perfect order they once were. Too much moving around to remain hidden, but we still have some on the matter. I believe the Sanctuary could provide some answers if given the chance."

"And what about the refugees? How will they feel, being cut off from their home?"

"Most seem inclined to stay here with gratitude. Some wished to join the fight and have done so."

I frowned. It wasn't the answer I had been hoping for. It was anything but.

There's nothing we can do, Zephyr said. *As much as it pains me to give that dragon yet another reason to think ill of my kind, I am in agreement with everyone here. For now, we need to have fewer portals open.*

I hadn't expected Zephyr to disagree with me since he'd experienced the same things I had, but here he was, telling me it wasn't a good idea. That we weren't strong enough yet.

I sighed and nodded.

"Okay. Let's get them closed and work out how to reconstruct the pillars," I said, hoping it was the right decision.

It's a decision. We needed to do something differently, Zephyr pointed out.

Everyone visibly relaxed, making it obvious that they had worried about my reaction. It was probably for the best right now. I didn't want to be a tyrant. They wanted the portals closed and the uncertainty to reduce. Somehow I would give them that. It was the only way.

CHAPTER SIX

It felt good to be in the air again, but I was tenser than I had ever been while flying. My mythicals and I were on our way to the Mexico portal to raid the library for useful books. Not that there was a library as such anymore, but a tentful of books had been hastily smuggled out or unearthed from the rubble the mountain had become.

We'd been to the Sanctuary and left Minsheng and Simon there to work out how the pillars were created. We needed a lot of information on the runes and the crystals that went inside them. The water crystal from the Texas site had proved useful too.

There was something missing, however: the power source that made the pillar strong. In one of the recent battles, I had kept a portal going by filling the elemental crystal in its core, but it had been almost bottomless. I could have stood there for days and barely added a percent to its capacity.

I had no idea how to replicate it or where that power had come from except for a memory Zephyr had about the greats using the power from their artifacts. It wasn't a perfect memory, however. There was a chance it was wrong, and they simply acted as conduits. The whole thing was confusing, even with the advantage of Zephyr's genetics.

The worst part, however, was how out of control this all felt. No matter what happened, I was always reacting, always stemming this tide or stopping that bad thing from happening. I was never standing at the top with everything beneath me safe and sound. I was tired of it. I had to do something.

We touched down outside a place that looked like a mountain rather than a collapsed heap of rubble. The elves who had been guarding it controlled earth, and I could feel them slowly moving it around, packing it in densely to make it hard for anyone who came through the portal buried under it.

As soon as Zephyr landed, Cherisse came out of one of the nearby tents and motioned for me to follow her inside.

"I think I've found something," she said. "Not sure without the memories in the big guy's head, but with any luck, it will do what you need."

Liking that she got straight to the point, I followed her inside.

My mood improved further when I spotted the platters of food beside the book she must have been looking through. I was going to like anyone who was willing to provide that much food for me and was helping me find what I needed, especially when she didn't want to be here doing this. She wanted to be on the other side of the portal, rescuing more refugees from the dark elf.

I had a final surprise in who was in the tent with her. Ruehnar and Aquilan were there doing something with a jar and some water, another set of books open beside them. They looked up as I sat by the food.

"Aella, we hoped you'd be here soon. I think we've found something that might help with creating pillars. Rather, with transferring the energy from an artifact to the crystal in the pillar."

Cherisse was frowning at me behind their backs, her eyes flicking between them and the books she had wanted to show me. I had to fight the urge to open my mouth and scream as loud as I could. This wasn't the day I had wanted or the result.

Before I knew what had happened, the jar had exploded, and the water was steaming. Aquilan reacted swiftly enough that the glass from the jar didn't get far or hurt anyone, but the water splashed as it boiled, and it took all my effort to stop it from happening.

Did you do that? Zephyr asked me.

I was sure I had, but it hadn't been intentional. I'd been biting my tongue and letting everyone else tell me what to do for so long that I wasn't sure if I could take any more of it.

"Sorry," I said a moment later.

"Didn't know you had that in you," Cherisse replied, the grin on her face making it clear she didn't care about me losing my cool.

It made me wonder what she had done that would lead her to be amused at my display and if it had been her or someone else in her mountain. I got the impression that asking wouldn't be helpful.

I grabbed one of the large sandwiches and took a bite before I considered tackling any new issues or being told what they had learned. The air and water masters from the Sanctuary quickly sorted out the damage, then came over to sit and eat with me.

Although I was ashamed of my reaction to their attempts to help me, I was grateful that they were all taking it in their stride.

"We'll soon have the portals closed," Aquilan assured us as he finished explaining what they'd discovered.

I was calmer now, but I still wasn't happy, and his words rubbed the open wound.

"I don't know if I want the portals closed," I blurted. "They have good behind them as well. We cannot keep running and hiding. At some point, we have to face Kirdash."

There were gasps as I spoke the name of the dark elf who was behind everything. That was understandable. It was clear he liked to get into people's heads and terrify them. He'd done it to me on multiple occasions.

"I hear you, but we're not strong enough," Cherisse replied. "I know you're Henera, but we've lost control. We've lost our advantage. We can't simply keep going and hope. We need to pull back and make sure we're using every advantage we have."

I wanted to growl. Cherisse had a point, but they were missing mine. The people on the other side deserved for us to do more. We'd left them there for a long time, and many didn't think well of us. As I thought this, I realized the irony. Cherisse and I had changed positions on the subject.

Before, she had been so intent on rescuing the others

that she had been willing to risk anything to get the portal open. Did I have any right to push for what was essentially the same thing because I'd talked to a dragon who was holding a grudge?

I didn't know the answer, but the elves took my silence for consent. They wanted the portals shut, so we would shut a portal. Then we'd need four large elemental-infused pillars.

Understanding what everyone was telling me made me want to pull my hair out as well as explode jars, but I was Henera. I couldn't endanger people by not controlling my emotions.

It was worrying enough that something had exploded because of me, let alone because I had grown angry.

You're overwhelmed. We've not had a break in weeks, and we're constantly on edge because we're expecting an attack. Anyone would be low on emotional capacity. Zephyr sent calming emotions my way, but I could feel his fatigue.

Kirdash was pushing us hard, and maybe everyone else was right. Maybe it *would* be better if we closed most of the portals again. Then we could fight through one on our terms and take a break afterward.

I focused as those in the room worked out what we needed to do and explained it to me. After another hour, I was left with one impression. Everyone was guessing.

They had theories about how the parts worked, but no one knew for sure because the endeavor required the elemental energy that was stored in one of the great artifacts. I subconsciously reached for the necklace about my neck. Tuviel's necklace.

While I was very sure I didn't need it to enhance the

mental component of my bond with Zephyr anymore, I remembered what had happened when I had first put it on; I had been able to hear Zephyr's thoughts. I had not been alone since.

I also knew that the four great artifacts, all of them on my body, had been significantly drained by making the first sets of pillars. I didn't want to drain them further, not when I still had a battle to fight with Kirdash. Or if I was not Henera, my descendant might.

Whoever faced Kirdash was going to need everything I wore. Of that, I was sure. I couldn't bring myself to trade one for the other.

"Are there more artifacts? Some that maybe aren't useful in battle?" I asked, interrupting an explanation on rune intricacies and how infusing them with elemental energy was more about being steady than powerful. Not that any of us had ever done it in either way.

"There are some, I believe." Aquilan looked thoughtful as if he were remembering one.

"We should locate one of each element, and we need to make the pillars and shut a portal," I replied.

"I can help there." Cherisse reached into a pocket and pulled out what looked like a small spoon. It was flat on the head end, and it extended. Where the top met the long handle, there were three blue crystals and a small paler one embedded in it.

"What does it do?" I asked as she held it out to me.

"Controls rain and makes it come closer to the user. Aids with weather control, basically. Previous leaders of Amcika used it to grow crops and either bring the rain to feed them or send it away, so the sun shone on them. It's not been used since an older Amcika elf made us some money, and we started using half-gnomes and dwarves to bring human food in and stored it."

I lifted my eyebrows; it was perfect. An artifact that wasn't needed here, although it might be useful in other countries. I wanted to take it to Minsheng to study it and see if he could replicate it. Instead, I put it on the table.

Aquilan added a ring that kept the wind in a small area calm. It was a trinket, but it was better than nothing.

"We need an earth artifact and a fire one," Aquilan said. "As soon as possible."

"There are rumors of a fire elemental artifact in a dormant volcano somewhere. Something that, well, keeps it dormant." Cherisse frowned as she spoke, not sure taking that one was a good idea.

Nuri know another. Great smithy used one to get his forge hotter. Made the belt you wore. Nuri help find it. Fly to it.

I didn't want to send my firebird away from me, but he sent me a quick mental image of a journey of so many miles that I wouldn't be able to fly it quickly or easily, even with human technology.

Go, I said. *Bring it back to us if you can, but don't put yourself in danger to get it.*

Nuri needed no more encouragement and flew out of the tent. As soon as he did, the familiar feel of our bond stretching tugged on me. I was going to be uncomfortable until he was by my side again.

None of the stretched bonds were as difficult to endure as when Zephyr was a long way from me, but straining them didn't feel pleasant. It would be impossible to talk to the firebird mentally after he was a certain distance away.

As my powers had grown, so had that distance, but I couldn't reach across thousands of miles. I was just going to have to let the bird go.

"So, earth elemental artifacts. Looks like I've got one to collect."

Cherisse got up again and went to the makeshift library, where some of the books were still stored in crates. She rifled through them, revealing many titles in old Elvish and something I struggled to read.

She stopped when she found one about a great city that had once existed.

"Mearlin," Cherisse stated. "Supposed to be a great elemental who helped a human become king and defeat an evil guy who wanted to murder lots of people. Or something like that."

"*The* Merlin?" I asked, then my mouth fell open.

"Mearlin. You've heard of him?"

"If the king he helped was called Arthur, or possibly Alfred, then yes. English mythology." I grinned.

"Fantastic. Looks like you know the guy. He was said to have a great ring that could be used to move the ground beneath the feet of riders. They traveled the length and breadth of the kingdom in almost no time. You don't need that. You can fly like the wind."

I grinned at the logic and how amazing it was to know that Merlin had existed and had been an elf. It made me wonder how many other myths were true. Had any of the Roman or Greek gods or the powerful demigods been mythicals? It made sense, given that I was bonded with a water pegasus.

I took the book and stuffed it into my pack. It looked as

if I were heading back across the Atlantic, although I wondered if it would be wiser to send someone else. At any moment, Kirdash could attack again, and I wouldn't let anyone else die because I wasn't there to defend them.

I was going to have to talk to Minsheng and figure it out. Enough people had come to harm. I had to put a stop to it.

CHAPTER SEVEN

Minsheng flicked through the book, reading sections here and there and making notes. I tried not to look too worried. He looked serious, and I wasn't sure I liked where this was going.

I was back at the Texas portal site, with Nuri so far away that I had a constant ache in the pit of my stomach. He'd gone south, but that was about all I could tell. The distance was so great that I wasn't sure if he was getting farther away or coming back. I just knew he was so far away it hurt.

Finally, Minsheng sat back and looked me in the eyes. I waited, knowing my Shishou would explain when he was ready and not before.

"You're going to have to go," he said, looking at his notes again.

"Surely any of the others could go instead," I replied. "Or a couple of them. It can't be that hard for an elf who knows what they're looking for to find it."

"I don't think the problem will be finding it, although

that might not be as simple as you think. There are loads of places in Britain that claim Merlin was there. This suggests Merlin was a trickster and a very intelligent elf. He hid his most treasured possessions behind riddles, puzzles, and what sound like elemental traps."

Gulping, I held out my hand for the notes. I didn't like the sound of this quest or that we might be walking into a minefield of elemental magic. If we couldn't get the ring easily, it might not be worth getting.

I studied the notes and shook my head, quick to realize it might be deadly even for someone of my skills and abilities.

"I think we need to find a different artifact," I stated as I got up.

"I don't know of any others. None that are any easier to find or so close. The elves and the mythicals who wielded these didn't leave instructions to find them. None except Merlin."

"Like he was daring others to test themselves?"

"Yeah. Or as if he knew that whoever came after them needed to be good enough to wield them."

I sighed. Despite wanting to send someone else, I got the message Minsheng was giving me. Merlin had made it hard to find this artifact, and that meant having the world's most powerful elf and her dragon search for it was the best option.

We can do it and come right back. Get the US to help us travel quickly again, Zephyr offered to reassure me.

I couldn't respond. I had buried so many mythicals. While I'd cared for some of them, of others, I'd had enough. I didn't feel as if I had any other option, though. We were needed in too many places.

With the instructions Minsheng put together for me, Zephyr and I flew to the nearest airport to go to the UK. I was cleared to land in yet another country, but I was also sure no one could stop me even without permission.

Whose army wanted to take on a flying dragon and the elf riding him when all we wanted was a single ring to save the world? Most countries wouldn't argue with us.

Despite that, I was nervous as we flew. I put it out of my mind as I looked at the notes I had been given, however.

There was an old castle, mostly in ruins, in the south of England, with a network of caves near it that were said to hold Merlin's treasure. Of course, humans had never found anything there, so it was all rumors and superstition. However, they had not looked the way we could.

The first test for entry sounded like an optical illusion. Without a doubt, it would have kept the human world at bay. It terrified me. Did I think I could do better than the other people trying to get to this ring?

If nothing else, we can just move the earth in the area and pick it up, Zephyr pointed out. *We need a rough idea of which direction to dig, though.*

For a second, I imagined my dragon standing at the bottom of a massive hole, using his powers to burrow deeper and moving the dirt to the side like an overgrown mole.

He shook his head but kept flying. I had Sen tucked into my jacket, and Roth was riding our slipstream. If I hadn't missed Nuri and been worried about everyone I had left behind, I'd have been happy. I loved being in the air and able to relax.

Instead, we had to fly hard and not waste our abilities.

The trip to the UK seemed to go more quickly since the notes took my mind off everything else. We touched down in the early morning light of another day, sleep making me feel better about what the hunt might bring.

Another advantage of the early hour of the day was our ability to go to the castle in question before the tourists who would visit it were awake or allowed in. I got the impression the staff wasn't keen about letting us in either.

Zephyr strode up to the castle in dragon form. There was a squeal, then nothing for several minutes.

I shouted our greetings, but no one opened the gate. I wasn't sure if we were allowed to break in or we needed to be careful who we upset while we were here. As I considered going into the castle grounds anyway, a car pulled up.

It was sleek, black, and reminded me of a vehicle I'd seen in Mexico. Iris got out, confirming my suspicion that it belonged to the organization.

"Minsheng said you were coming here to find another artifact," she called as she hurried up to the gate.

Not sure what to do or say, I nodded.

Without another word, she knocked on the gate in a complicated pattern. It might have been the beat of a song, but if it was, I didn't recognize it.

The person on the other side of the gate must have, however. There was a shuffle and a clank, then it swung open.

"Hello, my dear," Iris said, her rich voice pitched high. It sounded almost overly cheerful. "I've got the friend I mentioned with me. Talented young lady and some of her companions. Going to find that treasure for you, as discussed."

The guy standing on the other side looked between Iris and me before examining my mythicals one by one.

"When you said you were bringing someone with a special talent, I thought she might be an archaeologist. I wasn't expecting..." His voice trailed off as he looked at me again.

"I'm Aella," I said, looking non-threatening. "And these are my bonded mythicals. We have ways to find stuff others don't. I want a particular ring from Merlin's treasure trove, but I don't care what happens to the non-magical artifacts in the same place."

"And you think you can find something?"

"The world depends on it, so let's all hope I can." I grinned.

It wasn't the most intelligent or tactful response I'd ever given anyone, but it was true. I *was* going to need it to save the world.

My speech had a positive effect on my host. He swung open the gate and encouraged me to follow him toward the sound of the ocean crashing against rocks and the caves we would begin our search inside.

I tried not to show my trepidation as we were led down a steep flight of steps carved into the cliff. There was a fence on one side and a rope on the other, but it wasn't ideal, and it was too small for Zephyr to descend in dragon form.

Despite my expectation that he would fly to meet us at the bottom, he took human form, making our host drop his jaw at the transformation. I stifled a grin and began the descent.

By the time I reached the bottom, my calf muscles were aching, not used to this sort of exercise. We flew to many places and boosted our efforts with air elemental magic. I'd never walked down so many steps. I was saving as much of my power as I could today, however.

It helped that Iris also seemed bothered by the long flight of stairs. Our guide was fine, as if he'd taken a gentle stroll down a country lane.

I looked for the cave. The sooner I found this treasure, the better.

"Do you want to point me in the right direction, and I'll get started?" I asked out of politeness. I could see the cave's entrance, and it matched the sketch in the notebook Cherisse had given me.

"I won't deny I was hoping to be involved in some way," the guy replied. "I can stay out of your way and follow you."

If Iris hadn't also looked hopeful about being allowed to join me, I would have told them no and gone on alone. When I remembered she'd shown up on many occasions and supported me and given me the tools I needed to win yet another battle, I couldn't say no.

"All right, you can join me, but I need you to be careful and stay close. I'll do what I can to keep you safe, but Merlin was a cranky elemental. He didn't care if this was deadly for normal humans. Or elves, from the notes I was given."

The guy gulped, but Iris nodded, lifting her chin a fraction higher. Not sure which of them had reacted in the wiser way, I turned toward the cave and made my way inside. Zephyr stayed close to me, and Sen perched on my shoulder.

Roth entered last, his hooves clopping in the residual water from the tide that swept twice a day. I lifted my hand and was about to create a ball of fire to light the way when Zephyr pulled a flashlight out of his bag and turned it on.

Frowning, I tried not to be annoyed that I couldn't show off. Instead, I created an air barrier around us. I didn't think it was necessary, but I didn't want to take any chances when I had two humans with me who would be hard-pressed to save themselves in a fight.

As we progressed, the water grew deeper. The floor sloped, and it worried me. Although we'd brought equipment to deal with adverse conditions and not use elemental magic, there was a lot of water. On top of that, the tide wasn't all the way in, and I didn't know how deep the water would get.

We moved slowly, my mind merged with Zephyr's, scanning the air, water, and rock around us for a sign that Merlin's treasure was nearby.

I stumbled and used my abilities to keep myself upright, but I wasn't the only one. We all lost our footing in the next few minutes.

Eventually, we came to a dead-end, the rock rising again, then tapering off. I thought I must have missed something along the way, but then my mind felt it—a flutter in the air to our right and up.

Glancing in that direction, I moved closer. Zephyr shone the light up there, but it looked like nothing but more cavern wall. Nothing that would have generated a puff of air.

I reached out with my mind; it felt like rock, but also not like rock. After picking up a piece of stone from the floor, I threw it at the small area, using my abilities to guide it and give it more force. It hit the strange patch of rock and went through it as if it were a puddle and gravity had pulled it.

"Did that ripple?" Iris asked.

Chuckling, I nodded. We'd found the first of Merlin's little tricks, and I had to admit I liked it. He'd made water appear to be and feel like rock.

Zephyr and I took control of it and pulled it apart, separating the rock from the water and breaking the odd bonds that held the two. The water drained, and the area became an opening. A faint light shone beyond it, making me lift an eyebrow.

It seemed there was a secret cavern, and it was lit.

Not sure what to expect but wary because the notes I had spoke of more traps, illusions, and oddities, I pulled myself up to see better. Zephyr gave me a boost to make it easier. He morphed the rock to add hand- and footholds for our companions.

Grateful he hadn't forgotten them, I pulled myself into the gap. It was tall enough that I could crawl through it. Thankfully, it didn't go far before it opened into a small cavern. Then it widened into another that was larger. This one had runes all over the walls, and they glowed faintly.

Careful where you stand, Zephyr cautioned.

I was wary, placing my feet so they didn't cross any of the glowing orange lines.

As the rest of our group caught up, Roth having to wait outside in the part of the cavern network, I looked around, taking in the beauty of the Elvish runes. It would have taken months to carve this many, even with Merlin's ability.

Iris got her cell phone out and took photos, but I was sure none of them would do the place justice.

Sadly, it was likely to be the only record of this room by the time we were done. Given the notes from Minsheng, I was sure I was going to have to destroy some of these, doing it in the right order at the right times. Minsheng had also made it clear that getting it wrong might lead to a spectacular array of outcomes, several of which ended in our deaths.

With any luck, I'd choose the right option.

CHAPTER EIGHT

Zephyr stood in the middle of the room with Minsheng's notes. We had added to them. I was still worried that we would blow everything up, but Zephyr had confidence. He read the runes far better than I did, and I wasn't about to argue with him.

Not sure if I should interfere, I waited until he was ready.

We needed to remove the runes, which would shut off various systems in the cave. We also had to make sure we didn't shut off the sections that kept the room safe.

As Zephyr moved over to the first rune, I tightened the air barrier I'd formed around us. If something did explode, I would do everything I could to keep us alive.

There was a brief pause as Zephyr took a deep breath, then he used his abilities to remove a rune from the rock. Within a second, that rune went dark, then another, and another until a trail had formed.

Nothing else happened, and the pair of us exhaled in unison. So far, so good.

Over the next few minutes, Zephyr continued removing runes, sometimes rubbing one out to stop a chain reaction before a previous rune had faded. The light in the chamber dwindled, forcing me to fetch another flashlight from our packs and turn it on.

For the most part, I wanted Zephyr to have a chance to solve this, but I also didn't want to risk hurting our companions. Iris had given us some insight into the runes I hadn't expected, but I got the impression that she took her role with the organization seriously.

Sen kept everyone's spirits up with her antics. The myconid bounced around and smiled and snuggled with everyone. I felt sorry for Roth, however. The pegasus was stuck on the other side of the wall in the main cave.

I'd tried not to worry about him as the morning wore on, and now we were progressing to the next stage. Zephyr destroyed the last rune he thought he needed to change, then stepped back. The final set of runes blinked out one by one until there was a single chain of the runes running outward from the center of the room.

I had no idea what this chain was supposed to do, but do something it would. Interestingly, what the runes that were no longer connected and active didn't do changed things.

The wall behind us and between Roth and us vanished. That allowed the pegasus to join us, and it revealed another path.

"We need to go carefully in this next section," I said to Iris and the castle owner. "I'm sure it's booby-trapped in a traditional sense."

They nodded, stepping back and letting Zephyr and me lead the way.

I reached out, hoping that despite Merlin's ability with elemental magic, anything he had altered would be noticeable. I wasn't sure I could detect triggers, but I was positive I had to.

Pressure plate, Zephyr said a moment later, pointing at a section of the floor that looked different. It was a cunning spot, although my elven eyesight was better than a human's, yet not as good as Zephyr's when it came to noticing details.

As I helped the others around it, I considered what we could do to make sure we saw it on the way back. Iris came up with a solution, marking the spot with lipstick to make it obvious.

Confident we would notice it later, we kept walking. The cave network wound even deeper. We were all quiet and tense, no one knowing what to expect.

We identified another trap, a bowl of acid on a ledge, ready to be pulled off by the thinnest of trip wires. Thankfully, I noticed that one. We removed the wire, and I used my abilities to carefully lift the bowl and remove the contents in a controlled fashion. Zephyr stopped a large boulder that threatened to squash us minutes after that.

I exhaled as he held it out of the way. His scales and armor had kept him from being hurt when it crashed into him. With our powers, we broke it up, leaving the pile of rubble beside the path.

We reached a bend in the tunnel that opened into a final room. There seemed to be nothing there, but the air ahead felt as if it were real and not real, there and not there.

I frowned, knowing Zephyr was feeling it as well.

An illusion? I asked my dragon since Merlin was famous for illusion magic.

I think so. The trick will be working out how to break it.

After cautioning the others to stand back and stay there, I took a step and felt around to make sure everything was where it was supposed to be. My feet didn't quite touch the floor my eyes could see. It wasn't far off, but it seemed like there was something different underneath.

Wary about going farther while essentially blind, I moved the air around to feel where it was forced around objects I couldn't see and where it went through areas I believed were solid.

It didn't take long to be sure that what we could see and what was there were two very different things. I had no idea how Merlin had set this up, and I was impressed. I envied his magic and wished the elf was still alive so I could talk to him.

I was sweeping the area again, moving a gentle breeze with my eyes shut to focus on it, when something large lunged toward my companions and me.

"Look out," I yelled, then realized it was a stupid thing to say. I moved the air barrier I was holding in time to block it, then blasted the creature back.

It snarled, making it clear we were unable to see a vicious beast, then got back to its feet.

Panic rose in me. We were all vulnerable.

"Back into the tunnel," I told Iris and our tour guide. Thankfully, neither of them argued. I was soon standing in front of them with an air barrier behind and in front of me, waiting for the unseen monster to strike.

Close your eyes again, Zephyr said. *It makes the creature easier to notice.*

I exhaled, feeling for it the way Zephyr suggested, but I struggled, my heart racing and my mind more worried about being eaten or letting it past me than where it was.

Zephyr blasted the creature as it lunged toward me again, knocking it off-course. It yelped and growled but caught the edge of my air barrier anyway.

My mind reeled, fighting to hold it steady under the unknown threat.

What do you think it is? I asked Zephyr as I closed my eyes. Sight was useless. Zephyr was right.

My heart slowed as I forced myself to take steady breaths and let Zephyr fight the creature. Although I was concerned that it, whatever it was, could hurt Zephyr, with his dragon scales and the armor he had on top, not much could do him serious harm.

I, on the other hand, was the opposite. My body was as squishy and vulnerable as the average human's, and I wasn't wearing armor. None of the sets we'd found had been remotely close to the right size.

Once I focused, I was able to help Zephyr blast the beast back and pin it in place while we figured out what was going on and where it had come from. I didn't want to kill it, but it seemed intent on hurting us.

We lifted the earth around us, pulling up rocks from below and making a cage. The beast continued to wriggle and try to get free, but we kept it pinned, my mind drawing on the helmet as I reached into my pack and touched it.

The extra boost of energy from the earth and air crystals the helmet bore helped me build the rock-based pen quicker. A moment later, Zephyr and I completed it, leaving air holes to keep the beast from suffocating.

It was dealt with for now, but when I opened my eyes, I couldn't see what we'd constructed or the beast within. All I could see was the illusion and an empty dead-end.

Is there another way out? Zephyr asked, moving slowly, blasting air out around him to make sure he wasn't about to walk into anything.

There was no way to be sure without exploring it. The cavern, real or fake, was too large to take in at once. We spread out as Iris and the guide poked their heads around the bend.

"Be careful, but I think the beast is dealt with," I told them. "We boxed it up for later."

Iris raised her eyebrows as the creature snarled. I heard its claws scratch the rock on the inside, but it didn't shift anything or manage to get out. Warily and with arms outstretched, the pair of them came back into the cavern.

We fanned out to cover the room, moving around natural rock formations as we found them. Much of it was different from what we could see, but we moved slowly enough not to stumble and hurt ourselves.

We were approaching halfway when Iris exclaimed, then reached and patted something none of us could see.

I was closer than anyone else and changed direction, blowing air around what might be a sturdy pillar.

"This feels manmade," Iris explained. "There are carvings on it. It's not smooth like the stalagmites we've passed."

"Be careful," I replied, thinking about how the runes in the cave could have blown up.

Iris took her hands off it and slowly backed up. I used air to trace the shape of the object and found it was a pedestal. I had to get very close and use delicate puffs of air to make out what it was, but it didn't appear to have anything on it but runes and a raised top.

Press the top, Zephyr suggested.

What if it's a trap like the pressure plate in the other room? I asked.

I think the monster we couldn't see was the trap.

It was a good point, but I reached into the pillar to see if I could figure out what would happen when I pressed the top. It appeared to have a mechanism that would trigger, but as far as I could tell, it would just deface some of the runes.

Given that they were on and probably powering something, Zephyr had a good chance of being right.

After forming an air barrier around us, I pressed it. At first nothing happened since it took time for the runes to fade, but finally, the illusion disappeared. We were standing in an ordinary-looking cavern with a rock box containing a creature.

Interestingly, as soon as the illusion faded, the creature settled down, no longer desperately trying to escape and attack us. I moved over to it as Iris pointed out a small opening to yet another tunnel in the back-left section of the cavern.

I peeked through the holes to examine the creature within, but it wasn't easy to see in the dark. I widened the gaps until I could see a catlike creature similar to the small sphinxes I'd seen in LA but larger. They had been female, but I got the impression this was a male, and it had been half-starved.

I pulled one of my energy bars out of my pack and opened it.

"Are you sure it can eat that?" Iris asked. "We can get it traditional fare."

"We've got three dogs onsite," our guide confirmed. "We'll bring it a bowl and some dog food."

I nodded and took some photos with my cell phone. The creature didn't like the flash, but I managed to take a decent picture and sent it to Minsheng. My text asked if Orthelo could give us any advice about what to do with the poor mythical.

For now, we had to leave it there. Zephyr and I took the lead again as we walked through the next tunnel. This one was narrow but tall, and it wouldn't have worked for anyone larger than us. As it was, Zephyr and Iris had to turn sideways to get through some sections.

There didn't seem to be any more traps, just the natural difficulty of the cave. Thankfully, it didn't take long to get to the next cavern. This one wasn't lit, but the flashlight Zephyr carried showed us a small alcove at the back, tucked behind a large stalagmite. It appeared to hold a chest or a box.

As she moved closer, Iris took out another flashlight and shone it on the object.

It had been sitting there for so long that the edges of the box had been covered by the slowly forming stalagmite and the stalactite coming down from the ceiling.

The tour guide went to reach in and take out the box, but I stopped his hand.

"If this Merlin guy is like his stories, there could be yet another trap," I told him and reached with my mind instead.

The tour guide gulped and backed up.

"I won't deny I'm glad it's you doing this," he said a moment later.

I didn't reply. The last three years of life had been like this, with me doing things others couldn't or wouldn't in the name of progress and victory. Not that I minded, but I was usually the person who went into danger first.

It wasn't easy to feel around the box since it resisted elemental connection in a way I'd not experienced. As far as I could tell, the box had been put into the alcove near some natural formations, and they had begun to swallow it. Time and the weather had done what they did best.

I loosened the rock around it with my mind and reached in to remove the box.

I slowly shifted it out, finding that it was heavier and bigger than I'd expected. Zephyr helped me, then he started to open it. We paused and looked at each other. There was no lock, nothing to stop us as far as we could tell.

"You might want to stand back," I warned our companions as I gripped the air barriers I'd wrapped around us.

Zephyr and I didn't need to say anything, the bond between us ensuring we agreed on the right moment to tip the lid back and look inside.

At first, we saw nothing but a pile of dirty rocks, but

that was just grime on top of something else. The interior of the box was slimy.

"Mold, perhaps?" the tour guide asked.

I pulled a water bottle out of my pack and controlled the water as I tipped it over the rocks. Not touching anything in case it was dangerous, I pulled away the dirt with my mind.

I wasn't sure I was making much difference at first, but Iris shined the flashlight on the contents, and the objects under the layers of dirt slowly revealed themselves.

There were jewels, necklaces, coins, and rings inside the box. I was sure there was also an elemental artifact calling to my mind to connect.

I continued to clean until the dirt was in the bottom of the box and the contents were on top.

"I take it that's worth a lot?" the tour guide asked.

"In monetary terms, yes. In terms of protecting this planet, this is invaluable," I replied as Zephyr reached in and removed the ring that gave off an elemental marker.

"Is that the ring you were looking for?" Iris asked.

I nodded. A brooch gave off a fire marker and two crystals, one red and the other blue, reflected their elements.

I took those as well.

"We don't have a license to take more than one thing out of the box." Iris frowned.

"I'm not leaving gemstones that can be used to power elemental attacks. Consider it me making sure the rest of this treasure is safe and disarming a trap if that makes the paperwork easier to fill out."

I shot Iris and the tour guide my best no-nonsense look. Although most other elementals would have no idea what to do with the crystals, I couldn't take the chance. They would be used to defend the planet.

"You know, some would caution you to think about why the rules exist. No one person should get to decide what happens and have all the power," Iris replied. Her voice was gentle, but I could see her studying me.

I held them out to her.

"If you want them, feel free to take them. I don't want them used to damage a hurting world."

Iris blinked.

"Keep them," the tour guide told me. "I'll tell everyone you left what you were supposed to."

CHAPTER NINE

I was back on the plane and settled with the four elemental objects before I thought about what they might mean.

We had found what we needed to, and we had two extra crystals and a brooch as well. I was sure they had a lot of power in them. They called to connect to my mind, but not so I could fill them. They could be used by anyone who found them, or maybe Merlin had intended the stash to be there for emergencies.

We couldn't be sure. We had to get back to the US and make sure the portals and the people defending them were safe, although we had not been away for long.

I also had to figure out what to do with the mythical creature that had attacked us. In the end, we had used tranquilizer darts to sedate it and brought it out in a large crate. Sen was on watch to make sure it didn't awaken.

I was exhausted, having drained my powers, and was rushing back to my friends with fear and worry in my heart. Nuri was still far away, too distant to communicate with, so I had no idea where he was or what he was doing. I hoped he would return to me soon.

We had been in the air for about four hours when the co-pilot came to where Zephyr, Roth, and I were resting.

"We've had word from the Mexico portal that they're under attack and have been for a while. The dark elf seems to be concentrating his attention and magic there. The earth elves are hard-pressed."

"Redirect us there, or get us as close as possible." I sat up, on edge. We were still hours from any of the portals, and that terrified me. What if we didn't get back in time?

"On it. The President thought it best as well."

I nodded as he left. I wanted to call him back and demand he make the plane go faster. Anything so we could get there sooner to help.

There was little we could do since the plane was flying at about the speed Zephyr could have, but I had never been good at waiting. I was sure I was needed, so I didn't want to be where I was now.

Deciding to get some sleep, I curled up next to Zephyr and let him wrap his tail around me. I wasn't tired, but any power I could regenerate would be useful.

The co-pilot woke me hours later.

"We're not far from the Mexican portal," he began. "But we're not authorized to land, so this is as far as we can go." He looked apologetic, but I'd half expected something like that.

Zephyr got up and shook as Roth came over to us.

"You're going to need to keep an eye on the beastie here," I said, handing the co-pilot my small pistol and the darts that went with it.

He gulped, and I patted him on the shoulder. Sen grinned at him as she bounded off the edge of the large crate.

"Take him to the Sanctuary and let them figure out what to do with him."

"Yes, ma'am."

I couldn't help but smile as we opened the back hatch on the plane and prepared to jump out. Sen was tucked into my jacket, and after Roth and Zephyr left the plane, I followed.

Although the aircraft hadn't been able to get us all the way there, I could identify the mark on the horizon that indicated the fallen rubble pile of the mountain the Amcika cult of elves had once lived in.

I wasn't used to it from the air, only from the road. When it collapsed, it had left a nasty scar on the terrain. I tried not to think about it since we could do nothing about it while we were fighting the dark elf and his minions.

If the earth elves were organized effectively and their magic wasn't needed to keep portals buried, we could have gotten the elves together and rebuilt the mountain. Until the dark elf was defeated, however, or all of the portals closed for good, their power was required for other tasks.

That said, the elves defending the portal needed a place to live, but they had only created simple dwellings on top of the rubble.

Zephyr carried me as we flew closer, Roth in our slipstream, with me helping him keep up with us.

I tried not to worry when I got close and didn't see anyone moving anywhere. The mound was as untidy as the last time I was there, which made me hope we had arrived in time.

When we were close enough, I reached out to feel what was happening. I could sense the control of an elf defending the earth.

Descending, Zephyr circled so I could merge my control and mind with the earth elves. I could feel the pressure they were under.

The dark elf was exerting his will around the portal and had made a space that allowed some of his elves to come through. The dark elves were fighting to push out farther.

I could feel elves defending, though not the multitudes I had left here to keep this portal safe. Had the rest run out of energy?

There was no way to be sure, but I had to do something to help. I didn't have long to do it. To start, I held on with the others and considered bolstering the support with earth elemental magic from my helmet.

I wasn't sure what the status was. If they were all close to being drained, I was likely to need the helmet to hold firm, but if they had elementals in reserve, I could probably get away with throwing some at this fight to get it done more swiftly.

After Zephyr landed, he morphed into human form, and we hurried to the first of the huts on the surface of the ruined mountain. Someone noticed us and Cherisse came to the door, then quickly ushered us inside.

I followed her into the dimly lit room and took in the group of elves sitting with her. Simon stood at the back of the room with a model in his hands, and he was moving tokens of people around with a frown on his face.

"The first wave of the cavalry has arrived," Cherisse murmured.

Simon looked up, as did a couple of the earth elves, but many didn't. Some were sleeping where they were sitting or lying. It made sense if they had been drained and Cherisse was keeping the mountain defended.

The dark elves had tunneled partway to the surface, and they were pressing to get control of specific pockets. On top of that, I could feel Kirdash. The dark elf was using his elemental magic through the portal to widen the area around it and push even more elves through.

I could see why Cherisse and Simon looked worried and had called for us. I sat down and focused, using the elements to tell me what was happening in places I couldn't physically see.

When I reached, my mind challenged Kirdash. He'd never spread his control so far from a portal before, and it made me worry that he was on this side of it.

I pushed against his mind as he reached for the group of earth elves, connecting to the helmet's crystals to boost myself and keep him from disrupting my bonds. I reached for the air to work out how many dark elves were here and if my worst nightmare had come true.

The dark elves were apparently not concerned about the air. A single weak air elemental was controlling it, and I easily batted her grip out of the way. That done, I felt around for more elves and counted them. There were twenty earth elves, and they were all pushing out.

On top of that, more were coming through the portal, and a spent dark elf backed out of the fight, retreated to the portal, and went back through it.

I frowned. It seemed like the dark elf had an endless supply of earth elementals, and he was doing everything he could to aid them. We needed help, but until it arrived, I was going to have to buy time. On top of that, likely only Zephyr and I would be defending soon. Everyone else was spent.

No wonder they had called for backup. I hoped some of our elves could recharge enough to help me hold the dark elf off.

When Kirdash latched onto my bonds, I was forced to focus on dodging his grip, pushing him back, and attacking him any way I could. It wasn't as easy without Nuri by my side, but I had the advantage of being a fairly long way from the portal and knowing Kirdash was not on this side of it.

We clashed for what seemed like an age while his dark elves continued to show up and find ways to push against our control or slip past it while we were distracted.

It was an extra strain each time an earth elf defending the mountain ran out of power and had to unmerge their mind from mine. It grew so difficult that if it wasn't for my helmet and how full the attached earth crystal was, I'd be struggling as well.

Fear that we couldn't hold off so many earth elves when they were backed up by Kirdash grew in my heart. One moment could mean the difference between holding the place and losing it. We couldn't give up what little advantage we had with the portals being mostly buried and easier to defend.

"More reinforcements," someone yelled. I didn't dare turn to look, but hope fluttered within me. I'd been holding the attackers off, not daring to move or speak, and I had no idea how much time had passed. I needed help.

Minds merged with mine, and I let them help move the power and focus to where it was needed most. While I pushed Kirdash away, the dark elf latched onto the new minds.

Again I pushed him back, and his mind retreated, taking his control and my pain with it. I exhaled, realizing how weak I'd become.

Cherisse woke up all the sleeping elves, and more minds merged with mine. The dark elves in the mountain were forced to give up and retreat. We didn't close the tunnels they had created but simply pushed them back through the portal.

Fighting was difficult. Dark elves constantly came through the portal, and all the new minds were fresh. Their attacks were less enthusiastic, however, as if now that the dark elf wasn't there, they weren't convinced that pushing hard against my mind and those with me was a good idea.

I didn't dissuade them from that thought, just pushed them until they fled back through the portal. The dark elves left quickly, not wanting to stay behind in the caves.

The elves with me unmerged and retreated as well, but I had to find out what the situation was and if the portal was safe. Had Kirdash done anything in particular before I had come along and made it harder?

Despite my fatigue, I stayed where I was and closed my eyes. The elves around me stirred, but I ignored them and everything else.

Kirdash had done something near the portal. It was incomplete, but it worried me. He'd had plans for this portal, and he'd been confident he could make them happen. He had not appeared to expect me to come here and thwart him.

I eventually had to give up and pull back since I was drained.

As I did, the strain of my bond with Nuri being stretched eased. The firebird was on his way back to me at a speed that made me want to sigh in relief.

"So, Henera," Cherisse said, sounding exhausted. "What progress have you made on shutting these portals? Have you come to save us all?"

"I've not made much progress, but you're welcome for me saving your elves and this mountain from what would almost certainly have been carnage," I replied, grinning as she faked being irritated at me.

"I want this portal shut. I want to know my people are safe."

"Do we have everything we need to create the pillars?" I asked, still nervous about the idea.

"Once your firebird gets here and you pony up whatever artifacts you've found, we're good to close this portal and create some pillars."

I nodded. It was time for us to make the attempt.

CHAPTER TEN

Although my firebird was still too far away to communicate, I felt more like myself. I was standing near a lab bench with Simon, the artifacts and the notes the elf had made about what it would take to shut the portal in front of us. It was hard to cope with this since Simon had been part of the group that had tried to open the portals in the first place, and he'd killed a friend of mine.

I was putting all that behind me, but then something would happen and remind me that this man didn't have anyone's best interests at heart but his. Right now, that was evidenced by him working on a project that was linked to opening the portals but not the major focus.

In the meantime, we were getting the crystals we needed; the rune-powered machine someone had created many centuries ago needed four of them. Powering them, getting them inside rune-covered pillars that could make use of them, and getting those pillars in place around a closed portal was no easy task.

It had to be done, however.

We had pushed back the forces of the dark elf, and he was no longer actively attacking any of the portals between our worlds. I had a moment to breathe and try to solve problems.

"What are we doing with this?" I asked Simon as he brought out the device to block elements he was making. It wasn't something I wanted to test, and it hadn't worked the last time I'd tried.

"Just take it with you and try it again," he replied.

I put it in my pocket, then looked at the other device on the bench. It was emitting a gentle hum. I'd seen it a couple of times before, the first time inside the mountain when we'd pushed back an invasion. Kirdash's forces had gathered around the device and were feeding it power.

That power had then been channeled into elemental crystals, which we'd then used to force them out of the mountain. I was grateful for all of them and thankful we had a spare set to attempt to recreate the pillars.

"We need to get the power from your artifacts into the crystals, then hook those up to runes," Simon said. "I don't need you around for that part, but you're our most powerful elf. I am sure this experiment will fare a lot better with you around to help."

I didn't respond, but I picked up on the undertones and what he wasn't saying. If this went wrong, I could keep us from blowing everyone up or make it go right again. However, this was in the best interests of the planet, so I was willing to do what was needed.

As Simon hooked stuff up, I tried to think of something to say.

"It's funny where we've ended up," I began, not knowing how to make small talk. "You were adamant that the portals were a good idea, and I was adamant that there was nothing of importance on the other side except a threat we couldn't face."

"And at least one of us was wrong. The threat on the other side is...formidable, even with you on our side. Of course, no one expected him to have so large a force."

"I was wrong too. There are others of importance on the other side. We've rescued some of them. We met a dragon as well."

I wasn't sure what had made me tell Simon so much, but he was listening intently, and he *had* spliced my DNA together. I wanted him to know his efforts had not been in vain.

I also wanted to know if he knew what we had found. From the way he blinked and looked up, he didn't.

"Another dragon? And he's not controlled by the dark elf?"

I shook my head and smiled.

"He's one of the gold dragon line," Zephyr clarified. "The ones who hid when the rest fought and did everything they could to stay out of the fight. They're still staying out of it."

"I can't blame them. We all thought that was a myth, one of those stories people told to make it sound like someone or something might rescue us and not the Henera no one could see coming."

"Looks like you got the Henera and not the gold dragons," I replied.

This made Simon chuckle, but he didn't say any more.

He just went back to his work with the device and the crystals. I tried to follow what he was doing.

"Well, I think the crystals are in place," he stated a moment later. "Would you mind charging them for me?"

I put my hands on the device where he indicated. It wasn't a perfect solution since some of the energy was wasted during transfer, but it was better than nothing, and I was sure it would eagerly take energy from me.

It wasn't right, however, and although I could feel the crystals in the machine, it wouldn't let me transfer any magic.

Simon continued to tinker, testing things while I stayed where I was and periodically trying again. By the time they were connected properly, we'd gained an audience. Cherisse and several other elves had come to see if we had achieved any useful results.

Since we planned to shut the portal soon, none of the earth elves added rock and earth to the mound around the portal. We were going to be making the portal inactive, which meant we would have to get to it from the surface. There was no point in unnecessarily tiring the earth elementals here by burying it and then unburying it again hours later.

Eventually, I was powering the crystals for long enough to prove my point.

"That's a good start," Cherisse said. "How long until we can power up the pillars and get the portal shut?"

"I don't see any reason why we can't do so as soon as Nuri gets back with the fire artifact. We can prepare in the meantime," Simon said. "We should shut the portal, then power up the crystals and get them linked to the pillars after, while the right elves hold the portal shut."

"You make it sound like a piece of cake."

I'd rather it was pizza, Zephyr said, making me chuckle and shake my head.

"You and your private jokes," Cherisse said, but I could see the delight on her face. Since she'd been to the other world and bonded with a mythical, she'd changed, becoming calmer and happier.

I helped pick up all the tech Simon needed, making sure we had all three of the artifacts. I worried that Nuri wouldn't get here in time with the other one, but I could feel him coming closer. It wouldn't be long until he was back in my head, along with the others.

Although I had bonded with him last, he was such a presence in my life that it felt wrong not having him there. I was going to be grateful when he was back.

It took about twenty minutes to get everything to the portal area. It was dark, having been buried under an entire mountain, but I could see where the dark elves had been attempting to tunnel out.

As we got closer to the portal, I could also feel the strong markers of Kirdash. There had always been something about the dark elf's control that left a feeling behind. It was unnatural, and the elements desired to be rid of it.

Trying not to think about that, however, I focused on the portal, the shimmering light making the area dance and come alive. The portals were stunning in their way, and had we not been scared of what lay on the other side, they would have been wonderful to keep open and use.

But it seemed my ancestors had been right; while the

dark elf lived, they were too dangerous. He would have to be faced at some point, but not until I was ready.

I helped set up the device again, connecting all the crystals and laying out the artifacts with Simon while Cherisse instructed the other elves to bring in four large boulder-like objects. I stopped and stared. They were like the pillars from before, but smaller runes had been carved on the outsides in intricate patterns.

Unlike the previous pillars, these had a small hole in the top the size of the crystals I would embed.

The next thirty minutes were taken up by discussions about the exact placement of the pillars and what it would do to the area around them. These would have a smaller sphere of influence than the previous set had, but they would do the job as long as we kept the mountain guarded.

We had no more elves or humans on Earth who wanted to open them, which should make it easier to keep them closed, but I still had no idea how well this would work.

By the time the pillars were in place, we were waiting for Nuri. I could feel the firebird on the edge of my mind and had tried speaking to him, but he'd given me no response. It was tantalizing, but no one could do much until he got here.

Once the pillars were in place, however, the earth elves appeared and began modifying the room, making it larger and more spherical.

I lifted my eyebrows as they worked.

"The pillar influence tears apart anything within it. We don't want the mountain collapsing on us because they rip a chunk out of it as soon as we activate them, do we?" Simon said when he caught my expression.

I could have hit myself. I hadn't considered that, but it was worth being sure about. He was right.

I had to resist the urge to chip in and help, but it was clear my elemental powers were going to be needed for the portal closing and setting up the pillars. From everything I'd been told, it wasn't going to be an easy task, and I had to be sure that I had the capacity for it.

And I needed Nuri. We all did.

I'm close, the firebird said, his voice quiet.

Relief flooded through me. Knowing he was on the way and feeling no pain from him was a good sign.

I have artifact, he added before I could ask. *Old and needs clean, but working.*

After sending him a wave of affection and gratitude, I told Simon and Cherisse the good news. With any luck, we'd have this portal closed and guarded soon, and there would be no opening it again.

The rest of the wait was even worse. Nuri got closer and my stomach settled, but my nervousness about what we were about to attempt grew. I wanted to have this over and done with.

Nuri flew through the tunnels, guided by our bond, and landed on my shoulder.

I gasped at the soot and dirt that covered the firebird's bright and beautiful feathers. In his grip was a small pendant, and he dropped it into my hand.

His wings appeared stiff as he folded them, aching from being outstretched for so long. Tiredness came off him in waves, and Cherisse was concerned as she came closer.

"Can we get some warm water and food to clean him and help him recover?" I asked.

The cult leader nodded and relayed the order to the nearest elf who was not doing anything. He took one look at Nuri and rushed off.

I handed the pendant to Simon and let him get on with his part of the task. I focused on the firebird; I carried him to a safer place and set him down.

Before the food and warm water could be brought to us, I pulled a bottle of water out of my pack, tipped some into my cupped hand, and held it to Nuri's beak.

Zephyr and Roth came up, and Sen bounded onto the table. We started cleaning the grime off Nuri's feathers. The firebird let us work, his body resting against one of my hands.

Guilt washed through me at what he'd done and what it must have taken out of him. This wasn't something I'd ever have asked of him, and it made me feel far more guilty than I had expected.

By the time the food and a warm water bath arrived in a shallow container, he looked better, but there was a lot of ash and dirt.

What happened? I asked as he dipped his beak into a bowl of seeds and suet, which would quickly replenish his energy.

Old great forge. Not dormant, but controlled. It was...restless when I took the pendant. Checked nearby. No humans were harmed. Not the hazard it once was.

I sighed, relieved but aware it had been hard for him.

It doesn't look as if you've stopped since you left.

Nuri didn't. Just to sleep.

Rest now. You've done enough, I replied, feeling even worse but continuing to clean him.

When I was sure he'd eaten and drunk enough and we had gotten off the dirt and ash, I let him be. We made a well in the spare clothes in my pack and put him in it, soft and warm in the dark bag.

I straightened and turned my attention to Cherisse and Simon.

"Let's close this portal, shall we?" the air elf asked.

I nodded. It was time to stop Kirdash from being able to divide us and attack so hard.

CHAPTER ELEVEN

I stood in front of the portal, feeling the opening and connecting to it along with the other elves. I wasn't supposed to close the portal, but I was there in case things went wrong or someone struggled, my mind merged with the other elves'.

Cherisse was among them, along with Erlan and two others she had hand-picked. I recognized them, but I had fought them the last time I'd met them, so I wasn't expecting warmth and hugs.

They focused on their tasks, the elf who had started opening the portals guiding her elves to close one. At first, nothing happened, but I could feel the strain on the link to the elements around the portal and see the grimace on Cherisse's face.

I worried as power drained from me as well. I wasn't sure I could keep backing them up and do what was needed with what would be left.

The drain lessened, and there was a pulse of light from the portal as the connection to the other world broke. In the same way we opened the portal, Cherisse and the elves with her pulled it apart, unraveling it and giving us all back some energy.

Our efforts went into controlling the speed and where the energy went. I reached for the helmet and poured energy into it, not wanting to waste it. I was too far from the device to use the surplus to power the crystals.

Finally, it was done. As a group, we moved back, holding the portal closed. When I was sure they were all stable and out of the range of the pillars, I hurried over to Simon and the device, leaving my mind merged so I could aid them if needed.

"Okay," Simon said as he lifted the artifacts and several wires. "Now you need to disconnect from the others and act as a funnel for the energy from the artifacts to the crystals."

I wasn't sure I liked the idea, but Zephyr stayed merged and gave me a nod. He had their backs even if I couldn't during this process. It was better than nothing, and it was necessary.

Encouraging everyone to stand well back, I put one hand on the device and connected to the artifacts with the other. I felt the draw of the device, but then the artifacts linked to me as well, and I drew their power out.

The flow of energy through me was almost painful as it moved up one arm, across my body, and to the next artifact. I didn't like it, but there wasn't a good way to stop now that it had begun.

I concentrated on keeping the flow regulated.

"Looking good so far," Simon said, his eyes on the crystals and what was happening on the device's end.

I wasn't going to contradict him, but the strange feeling in my body continued to grow, and I wasn't sure it was a good thing. Not long after, the pendant Nuri had retrieved hummed and vibrated.

"I don't think it's supposed to be doing that," I said as the pain intensified. It felt like a fire was burning inside me.

I fought to slow the process and take control of the heat within my body, cool myself, and make it lessen and not hurt my bonded mythicals.

"What's happening?" Simon asked, his voice higher in pitch.

"It's like it's leaking," I replied, not sure how else to explain it.

"The crystals are almost there. Keep it going."

I nodded, but the connection to the fire artifact was changing as it grew more agitated. It started pulling energy not just from me but from everything around it. It was heating my body, and it was starting to heat the air around it as well.

Zephyr stepped closer, merging his mind with mine to help me control it and its impact. Simon waved the other elves over.

"Let's get these crystals ready," he said. "I think we're going to have to install them fast."

Gritting my teeth, I considered telling him he should have had them prepared, but I had to concentrate since the pain continued to get worse. Zephyr helped, but the artifact leaked power and there was nothing we could do.

I tried to stop the process to check everything, but it wouldn't let me. Sen even bounded toward it, her dragon scale armor glowing, reflecting the light the pendant gave off. It was disconcerting. She wiggled the connection to the artifact to see if that helped.

It made a difference, but not much. The artifact continued to create heat until sparks were flying. The device channeling the power into the crystals started heating up, making me wonder if something wasn't working on that end.

All the artifacts were behaving strangely, and the device was giving off a high-pitched whine. The crystals started pulsing. The pain grew more intense, forcing me to shut it off and disconnect.

It was too late. Zephyr wrapped his arms around me and pulled me away as Roth and Sen leaped clear. Something exploded, the noise making my ears ring. I flew backward, slamming into the ground in Zephyr's arms. I grabbed the air and slowed the objects moving in it, hoping that protected the others.

I stayed where I was, my body hurting, my ears ringing, not sure I understood the destruction. The fire artifact had exploded. The device channeling power into the crystals had done a good job of exploding with it, and one of the crystals I'd been filling was shattered.

I wasn't sure which of the three explosions had sent us all flying, but everyone had been propelled backward. When I looked behind us, the pillars the other elves had been getting ready had fared almost as badly. Two of them were broken, while the other two had been pushed back.

Around me were charred bits of table, rock, electronics, and injured elves. I wasn't sure where to even begin help-ing. I checked my bonded mythicals first, feeling for any injuries that weren't mine. Sen had a pain in her chest, but she let me know she was fine.

When she got to her feet, I gasped. A sliver of metal from the fire pendant was sticking out of her armor, smoking, charred, and sharp.

She stared at it, and I was again grateful to Daisy for making the armor for Sen. It had saved the myconid's life.

Cherisse came to my side, limping but waving away the medic who came rushing in.

"Go help one of the elves on the ground. They probably need it more," she said as she moved to the table.

"What went wrong?" Simon asked as he got up, looking unharmed apart from singed eyebrows and dirt on his pants.

"I was about to ask you the same thing," Cherisse replied.

"Either the device or the artifact didn't like something," I explained. "The connection between the two wasn't right to start with, and it leaked and got worse. Hurt like hell."

"Well, we've got neither now, and we're down a crystal again. We're not blocking this portal today." The frown on Cherisse's face deepened as we realized the enormity of her words.

We'd expended an artifact and broken the one thing that could create the crystals and pillars. Stopping Kirdash had just gotten a lot harder.

"We need to bury this portal again until we figure out what happened. I'll stay here for a day or two to help work it out and talk to the Sanctuary about organization. Maybe we can figure out what went wrong and fix it," I said, but I was as disappointed as Cherisse.

My heart ached for Nuri, who had flown so far and used so much energy for an artifact that had been destroyed. It didn't feel right that one so difficult to get had broken so easily.

I collected the other three artifacts. They were singed, but they still appeared to work, although they seemed *less* somehow. Energy had drained from them, making them less effective.

Nuri flew to my shoulder. Once I had them stowed in my pack and had helped a medic elf work the shrapnel out of Sen's armor, I surveyed the area again. It was clear that it was going to take a while to get everyone out of the mountain, with several elves injured. This shouldn't have happened.

With the dark elf and his forces constantly attacking us, we couldn't afford the things we were doing to protect ourselves leaving elves hurt and drained too. It wasn't worth it.

We were trying what we thought was best, Zephyr said, the voice of reason.

That doesn't make it easier to see injured elves. We caused that.

Not intentionally. There was nothing we could have done. You controlled everything as well as you could. We don't even know why it didn't work or what failed.

I frowned, not sure that was good enough. If we tried something like this again, I wanted to understand every last element of the process to make sure it couldn't go wrong. I would not let elves in my care get hurt again.

Although I wanted to do more to help the injured elves, we had to close all the tunnels and bury the portal again. It wasn't going to be easy, and it was going to take a long time. The least I could do was get a head start.

As the medics worked and Simon took away the wrecked device and his other equipment, I joined my mind with Zephyr's and several other earth elves'. We began shifting the rock, closing the gaps the dark elves left behind.

Still angry, hurt, and processing, I worked for what felt like hours. The portal room emptied long before we got to the point of making the cavern smaller and closing it. We slowly backed out to the surface.

During the ascent, we were brought food. More came to help us or left us as their powers ran out. I worked so methodically and with the aid of so many elves that I continued on for hours. My feet hurt, and I lost track of the time of day.

I think we should rest, Zephyr said when I yawned. *We've pushed a lot today, and Sen and Nuri are in need of attention, food, and rest.*

I wanted to argue, but we were low on power. The pain I was feeling from standing for so long was transmitting across the bond. It was time to stop putting my bonded mythicals through that.

Feeling guilty, I unmerged my mind from the other earth elves' and pulled back. I was no good to them tired, but I was determined to be back to finish the job soon. This world was going to be safe from the dark elf if it took all my strength and determination to make it so.

I went to find Cherisse and Simon after I ate, knowing Simon would be finding answers and Cherisse would want them. Wherever they were, they would be together.

I encouraged Sen, Roth, and Nuri to rest, and Zephyr came with me to find the elves. They were in one of the nearby huts, looking at broken pieces Simon was hooking up to strange-looking bits of lab equipment.

"Ah, Aella, you could be of use. I've almost worked out what went wrong, but I need some elemental help to be sure." Simon motioned for me to put my hand on the panel that had once been on the side of the device. It was beside it now, but wires ran from it into the partially repaired device.

Tired but willing to try, I connected with the object. It was unresponsive at first, but eventually, I could feel elemental energy flowing slowly out of my hand into it.

Simon picked up a small box that was taking measurements and nodded, apparently seeing what he'd expected.

"What is it?" Cherisse asked before I got a chance.

"The device is working perfectly. The problem was the artifact. It had become unstable, either through time or heat, or it didn't have enough energy left for what we did. It leaked, then the heat from the leaking made it worse until it blew up. It made everything around it unstable too."

I exhaled, glad Nuri was sleeping and didn't hear that the trip to get the artifact had been wasted.

"Was there anything we could have done to stop it or detect it before we charged the crystals?" I asked seconds later.

Simon paused and looked thoughtful. I saw a lack of concern on his face. He had no remorse for the elves who had been hurt today. In contrast, Cherisse looked as if she would murder him if Simon gave the wrong answer. The object of her wrath was oblivious.

"We might have been able to. It wasn't something I thought to test. The artifacts were created by the greats or craftsmen of a skill level we struggle to match. They're generally infallible."

"Then you might want to make sure you check every tiny detail the next time we try anything this important because I want to know beforehand if there is a risk or something might not work. I don't want every strong elf we have in the danger zone, not prepared or consenting to face that level of danger." Cherisse spoke quietly, but the bite in her words was clear. She was angry at Simon.

Knowing I didn't need to say anything helped me calm down as I disconnected from the machine. There was nothing more to do except rest. We would figure out if a second attempt was even possible in the morning.

CHAPTER TWELVE

It was easy to despair as I sat at a table with Cherisse and focused on a screen. Minsheng, the general from the Texas site, Sierrathen, the major from the California site, and the President were in video boxes in front of me. None of us knew what the best solution was.

"Simon is sure we can try again if we find another set of artifacts, but he recommends we consider the Texas portal if we make another attempt," Cherisse said, to rescue the melancholy of the discussion.

I admired her optimism, but I didn't share it.

"I can see the sense in doing so. The Texas portal is the hardest to defend, and we don't have to unbury it to make the attempt," the President replied. "But we cannot afford to repeat the failure."

"I won't do it again until I'm sure we have everything we need exactly how we need it. I almost lost Sen. Nuri exhausted himself to get the artifact, and that was just the personal cost. Too many were injured." I growled the last few words, letting my anger wash over me.

It was enough to convince the others to give it a try. The President nodded.

"Okay, we need another fire artifact, one we are sure works. We also need to find more to close the other portals or a way to replicate them."

"I might know of a fire artifact. It was told to me in a child's story by my mother," Sierrathen said. "A small ornate pouch that could warm any room in a matter of minutes or keep elves from the cold. There were several of them when the Sanctuary resided somewhere far colder with harsh winters. I have pinpointed the location. It might be a good place to visit and explore."

It wasn't a perfect option, but we didn't have many alternatives. I needed to find another artifact, and soon.

"Okay, let me know the location. If I could borrow a plane to get closer, that would be helpful. I'll go find it. Everyone else, protect your portals and get the Texas one ready to close. I'll come back as swiftly as I can."

I got up as if I were done with the conversation and ready to go, but as I did so, I saw the President and Minsheng blinking at me. I realized I'd given a command and made it clear that I thought I was in charge and calling the shots this time. It was the first time I'd given the President an order, and I wasn't sure how he would take it.

"You heard Aella," he said, a slight smile passing across his face as he spoke. "Let's get back on track."

That satisfied everyone who had hesitated. Everyone logged off. Sierrathen forwarded the location. I frowned. It was in Greenland, at the most distant edge of the south coast. Yet again, I had to go a very long way to get something I wasn't sure I needed or would be there.

I was leaving everyone in danger while I did it, not to mention the toll all this was taking on my mythicals. With no hope that it was going to get any easier but knowing I had to try something, I made my way to my hut and repacked my bag. We were going to need a lot of snacks.

Can we get pizza on the way? Zephyr asked as we woke everyone up.

I laughed and nodded. We had to fly to the US border to get on an aircraft, and I wasn't sure how far it could take us. That meant we needed to be ready to fly on our own. There was no better way to make sure we would cope than make pit stops for good food along the way.

We were all grateful when the weather proved to be calm and clear. There was nothing worse than flying through a rainstorm or anything dangerous. I could keep us safe, but it was taxing, and it took the fun out of flying. It was better not to waste our time and energy on that.

Thankfully, someone in the US Air Force had decided to make our lives easier, and when we arrived at the rendezvous airport to get on the plane, there was a large stack of delivery pizzas waiting for us. I grinned as we rushed over to dig in, Zephyr changing from dragon form to human so he could enjoy the fare more easily.

It was heaven to eat as we flew. The co-pilot let us know how far we could go and how long it would take. I was on edge, waiting for other people to do their thing while at any moment, Kirdash could attack again. I wasn't getting better at being patient and not worrying. It was a hardship to endure repeatedly.

I saw Greenland on the horizon and below us as the plane descended. It wasn't ideal to land in a foreign country, but the UK and Ireland had been accommodating so far. Hopefully, Greenland would be as well. It made me grateful I didn't need the cooperation of a politically charged country like Cuba or Russia.

When the plane touched down at a small airport, there was a group of important people in suits waiting for us. Trying not to appear intimidated, I got out of the back of the plane and smiled at them.

"I'm Aella, and these are my mythicals. Thank you for letting me visit your country. Some friends of ours believe that they left something here a long time ago and wish to see if I can find it."

"We have been so informed by your government," the middle guy said, stepping toward me. "This is a strange request to make of another country."

"I'm aware. I know we shouldn't be making demands, but whether Earth likes it or not, we're at war with the dark elves on my homeworld. Kirdash doesn't care about borders or fighting as you know it. All he cares about is whether he is getting what he wants. I'm trying to stop him. I need something that might be here."

No one reacted to this either positively or negatively, so I stood my ground. It was awkward, but I couldn't afford to back down. I might not be the perfect leader, and I might not have all the answers, but I was protecting the entire planet. That had to count for something.

"We can take you where you need to go. I hope you understand we do this in the interests of protecting everyone. We don't like being dictated to, and we don't feel the threat is ours as much as yours."

"Understood," I replied, keeping my mouth shut.

We don't have to like them, Zephyr said, reminding me of a very good point.

I focused on the task I had at hand as the small entourage led me toward Customs. They exchanged words in a language I didn't understand. It wasn't easy waiting when the other portals could be attacked at any moment, but it couldn't be helped.

Thankfully, we were ushered toward the exit shortly, and my mythicals and I were escorted out into the morning light.

There was a large, open-top vehicle waiting there. Several soldiers stood at attention, with a couple more seated in it and one driving. I hid my frown at their display of power. It was awkward but also funny.

The soldiers wouldn't have been able to do anything to stop us if we'd wanted to attack. It was a waste of their resources, but if it made them feel safer, so be it.

As soon as my mythicals and I were settled in the back of the vehicle, along with several of the dignitaries, the other soldiers climbed in, and it pulled away.

"I understand you are looking for an item of value within our country," the leader said.

"It has value, yes, Mr...." I replied.

"Please, call me Niko Jansen. I do not understand your response. An item has value, or it does not. The exact value is perhaps open to debate, but something is worthless or not."

"I'm looking for a device only an elf can use. It has no value to anyone who cannot use it." I fought to keep the bite out of my voice, not sure why this guy was being so obtuse.

He's going to want the US government, or us, to pay for it, Zephyr said. *There have been a lot of men like him in history.*

It might not be him. He'll have a boss.

True. Can I eat him then?

Maybe we can make it a part of the negotiation. Give us the artifact, and the dragon won't eat anyone. Does that seem like a fair offer to you?

If I get pizza when they choose not to let me eat them.

You had pizza a few hours ago.

I know, but by the time we've found this artifact, I'll be hungry again.

Our banter improved my mood, although it earned me strange looks from our escorts. I didn't have to make them like me, just get what I came for.

I spent the next few minutes describing the artifact and what it could do.

"And providing this heat is somehow important for the human race?" Jansen asked, not sounding convinced.

"No. I want to drain the artifact of its power and use it to power something else. Something that can be used to keep a portal to the elven homeworld closed."

"You want to close the portals?" the man asked, his surprise not coming from where I expected it to.

"Yes. The dark elf and his followers on the other side have the power to murder every person on this planet or enslave them. I am trying to prevent that." It was an exaggeration. I didn't think the dark elf realized there were over seven billion people on Earth, and a fair few of them were able to fight back.

The diplomat didn't respond, and silence fell. The suits

glanced at each other, which made me wonder if they knew what we were saying.

Zephyr took advantage of the silence and diplomatically asked about the country. It gave me time to calm my nerves and reach out with my mind. Something wasn't right, and if I was going to find myself in trouble, I wanted to be ready to defend us and fight back.

The journey took over an hour, but Zephyr's attempts to be polite had a positive impact on the demeanor of our escorts. They perked up while talking about their country with pride, and it made it easier to focus on what might be going on but also relax.

Everywhere we went, the air felt clean, and the elements were unmarked. This place wasn't controlled by anything, and if there were elves in the country, they weren't active.

I stilled the alarm bells in my head and focused on finding the artifact. We weren't far from the location Sierrathen had given me, a small GPS device on my wrist letting me know it was nearby. I didn't want to miss it, so I reached out with my mind.

The diplomats glanced at my wrist several times and then at Zephyr, noticing my distraction, but they didn't say anything, and the driver kept going.

They took an interesting route, however, not going straight to the area, but taking two sides of a triangle when the third would have been more direct. Without knowing what the roads were like, I wasn't sure if it was deliberate or not, but by the time I realized that was what they were doing, we were almost at our destination.

Reaching into the area we'd missed, I felt for anything

hidden there, not trusting what was going on. However, everything I connected with was as clean and unsullied as the rest of the country had been so far.

Zephyr merged his mind with mine, making it clear he had similar suspicions. The increase in power gave our range a boost. We pushed out farther as the car came to a stop near an area of wilderness and forest.

I wasn't sure if I was being paranoid, but something felt as if it were using or controlling a fair amount of elemental power right on the edge of our range. There was no way to expand it without another air elf.

As we got out of the car, I slipped my hand into Zephyr's. Something wasn't right, but for now, there was nothing we could do about it.

Let's see if we can find that artifact, Zephyr said. *One problem at a time. None of them appear to want to hinder us or hide anything. Maybe we can let them keep their secret.*

True. As long as we find the artifact.

I sighed when the dignitaries looked at me as if they were expecting me to put on a magic show. If the situation hadn't been so strange, it would have been funny, but today I was tired, unsure what I'd gotten myself into, and eager to be back in my country to protect the people I cared about.

I had to find one little object. In a forest. Where it might be buried by time and age. If it even still worked.

CHAPTER THIRTEEN

We spent an hour moving back and forth across the area, reaching out with our minds and abilities to find evidence of the artifact, old Sanctuary dwellings deep under the earth, or anything that indicated we were in the right place.

I was beginning to despair as our path got farther out in a circle from the coordinates Sierrathen had given me. The soldiers accompanied us on the walk. The diplomatic types had given up when they realized we were going to be searching in ever-increasing loops, but the soldiers had stuck by our sides the entire time.

This wasn't working, but I didn't know what else to do. It didn't feel like any structures had ever been here. The ground was free of signs of old buildings or elemental markings.

I came around to the side of the circle nearest the coordinates we were seeking, and the soldiers tensed and glanced at their superiors. I found nothing, however, and I didn't want to waste my energy discovering their secrets or make my hosts angry when I needed an artifact.

We went around again, still finding nothing. My legs were tired, and my feet were sore. This wasn't working, but I couldn't go home empty-handed.

Go around again, Zephyr said. Roth walked over to drink from a small stream as we tromped through more trees. *I might have felt something, but I'm not sure. If we can go near that section again, I can be sure.*

I wasn't going to argue with the first sign of hope we'd had since we got there despite how weary I was. If we didn't find anything, I could take a break after another loop. If nothing else, it was interesting to see who showed tiredness first.

As we came around again, getting closer to the secret the diplomats had, they were more agitated, and the soldiers gripped their guns tighter.

There, Zephyr said, drawing my attention to something under the ground. I stopped and followed where his mind was probing. It was the shape of a small hut, and beside it was what felt like an old wall. We walked toward it to get a feel for what it might be.

I wasn't sure if it was human or elven until I felt the faint marker of an earth elf in the depths of the wall's smooth base. There was a construction deep underground that an elf had made.

As we stopped above the hut, Roth, Sen, and Nuri with us again, I realized the diplomats had left their spot by the car and come toward us. A couple of them wore frowns, which puzzled me.

We're getting closer to their secret, Zephyr pointed out. *It feels as if this wall leads in that direction.*

Neither of us dared look that way, so we focused on the

ground. I closed my eyes and delved deeper and around the hut. Although there was the faint feeling of an elf-made building, there was nothing as strong or obvious as an artifact.

"Have you found something?" the diplomat asked. "Something we could dig up for you?"

"Oh, I don't need you to dig. If you stand back, we can do that. Yes, we've found something that was made by an elf a long time ago. Would it be a boon to your country for us to uncover it despite our artifact not being in this building?" I asked, keeping the focus off their secret.

I received raised eyebrows, and they glanced at each other, so I decided to show them what I meant. I reached into the ground and, with Zephyr's help, moved it out of the way until I'd revealed part of the long wall and the base of the hut. There were items of pottery, old tools, and everything else a person might find in an archaeological dig there too.

Grinning, I pointed them out, making it clear that I could feel the markings of an elf on all of it.

This made one of the men more animated. He'd not said a word to us so far, but now that he could see something for our efforts, he seemed genuinely interested and asked me what I could tell him.

Knowing it might win me an ally later, I told him everything I could about the hut and what we'd found, using my magic to glean info others might not. Zephyr added things he knew from ancestral memory, and we painted a picture of the likely use of the hut as a single elf's watchtower or guard station.

As soon as that was done, I moved to the wall and

uncovered more of it. My excavation led toward the mysterious location, and once again, there was concern on the faces of everyone with us.

"I need to follow this wall," I said. "Do you want me to reveal it as I go, and any other structures we come across?" I asked, sounding innocent about what lay beyond. I didn't want them to know I had picked up on their deceit and subterfuge.

There were more looks between them, but a nod was enough for me to assume it was safe to continue. I turned my attention back to the wall, and Zephyr and I moved the earth to one side and uncovered it as we walked.

As the day wore on and we made slow progress, I got hungry, but I didn't have any food with me, and it didn't appear that our colleagues had any either. I got the feeling that they hadn't expected this little mission to take so long.

We kept going for several hundred yards, and I was sure I could feel something magical ahead. I stopped and drew Zephyr's attention to it.

"Is there any way we could get some lunch?" I asked as Zephyr probed deeper. "Is there a takeout place that could deliver? It's hungry work using magic, and we have not found anything but a wall."

I think we've found a road, Zephyr said, still examining the object.

Now we were closer, it was obvious what it was. We could feel the old settlement under the current buildings and the unmistakable elemental connection of an open portal. I frowned as our minds touched on the control of another air elf, someone in the vicinity who was patrolling.

If anyone noticed us, they didn't say so, but we withdrew our minds now we knew the big secret. There was a portal nearby. It was active and guarded.

The soldiers made a call to get us lunch, and I sat beside the uncovered wall and what might have been a road beside it. It wasn't ideal, but it provided shade as we waited for food and gave our abilities time to recharge.

Although we didn't have to reveal the wall, it had been necessary to show the people with us that we were following the trail to the portal they were hiding, so they didn't think anything else was happening. I was very concerned about finding yet another open portal.

I assumed no one had attacked through it, but it was only a matter of time. If the country didn't know what danger they were in, I was going to have to make it clear. Not that I knew how to do that, but I had to get to the point where they dropped the pretense first.

The food arrived, an array of different dishes. Some of the diplomats took the opportunity to walk away from us and make calls while others talked to us, asked us questions, and made a fuss over Sen, Roth, and Nuri, no doubt to distract us.

Do you think we should put them out of their misery and ask if they've had any trouble with the portal? I asked Zephyr when we were almost full. His mouth twitched, but no one appeared to notice his mirth or our conversation.

Maybe, but it is so funny to watch them hide it. It does give us the upper hand, though.

It does, but they're doing everything they can not to tell us.

We're going to have to get close to it soon. It's likely the artifact is near it or possibly on the other side.

The latter thought made me pause partway through

telling one of the friendlier men about Sen's ability to create ice darts and control vines. It drew looks my way.

"Sorry," I said. "All of us are aware of what the others are feeling. Our bonds are very strong, and sometimes it's distracting when one of us feels something intense. We're all fine, though."

I got more strange looks, but I decided enough was enough. The diplomats all came closer.

"Right. Shall we continue on toward your portal and see if our artifact is on this side or the other?" I asked. Many of them gaped, and one of them glared at another. "I can feel it. I've known it was there the entire time. I don't care about the portal, just the artifact, like I said. It's clear you're worried about it for some reason."

"You can feel it?"

"Yes. The same way I can feel the remains of the road the elves created below and the remains of the buildings up ahead. I will be able to feel the artifact when I get close. Elven creations leave a mark other elves can feel."

"But we're still half a mile away."

"I'm the second strongest elemental elf in history, and I'm getting stronger. That brings me to my first question. Who opened your portal, and does the dark elf know about it?"

The men exchanged looks, then Jansen sighed and decided to stop hiding their knowledge from me.

"We've not had the dark elf come through it, nor any attacks. I don't know why not, given what you speak of. It's been open as long as we've known of it. It was buried underground and was discovered by our archaeologists several years ago. We didn't realize it was a portal and related to your kind until last year."

I nodded, understanding a lot more.

"What did you fear would happen if I found out? If the dark elf doesn't know about it, I'm not going to draw attention to it. If it has never been shut, or it was opened a long time ago, then it is probably one of the safer ones for now."

"We know the US government acts as if it controls the portal found in Mexico. That is a constant source of difficulty for the Mexican government. They wish to protect their people and not be beholden to the US and their interference. This is *our* portal."

"Okay. Well, first, it might seem like the Mexican portal is owned by the Mexican and US governments, but in truth, it's owned by neither. It's in a mountain that elves have occupied for over two thousand years, and if you asked them, they'll tell you it belongs to them and point out that you'd die trying to take it from them. I know. I and almost every other elf I know discovered that the hard way."

That caused more raised eyebrows, but I didn't stop there. It was clear that these folks needed an education about the forces they were dealing with. They didn't understand them or what was truly going on.

"Second, no one wants to take this portal from you, just protect the planet. If you think you can handle stopping a dark elf invasion through it, then I'm going to let you handle it. One less portal keeping me awake at night sounds amazing."

"How bad are the attacks?" Jansen asked.

I frowned, sure their portal must be hidden for now. These folks had no idea.

"It took about sixty percent of the world's most powerful elves to keep the last one at bay, bearing in mind that I know about less than a thousand of us. It took over twelve hours to fend off and another twenty-four hours after that to make the defenses strong again. We lost two elves in the battle. It wasn't even the enemy's full forces. It was also our most easily defended portal."

Their faces paled as I spoke. I felt guilty for scaring them, but it was necessary. They didn't understand what they were up against.

I continued to explain, demonstrating my abilities with help from Zephyr. We simply walked the rest of the way to the portal. Since we no longer bothered revealing the wall along the way, it took about ten minutes to get to the large building over the portal.

There was a ramp to the front door, which was on a lower level and set back from a fence.

It was clear that nature had been reclaiming the area. I detected more buildings, so an elven settlement had been here once. There were nowhere near enough for it to have been the Sanctuary.

I think it must have been on the other side of the portal, Zephyr said. It was apparent that there was no artifact over here.

"I'm going to need to go through the portal. The city I'm looking for and the magic it contains must be on the other side," I told the diplomats.

"I don't know if we can let you do that," Mr. Jansen said. "You shouldn't even know it's here."

"While I can appreciate you being in a difficult position, I don't think you understand. I know there's a portal here, and I need an artifact this city holds to save the world from a threat far more powerful than any of us. That said, I'm also powerful enough that I could kill every single one of you right now, and not one of you could stop me. Believe me, guns won't save you when your bullets won't even reach us. Feel free to shoot at Zephyr or me to find out."

One of the soldiers lifted his weapon, and Zephyr gave him his attention.

"Go on. Shoot me," my dragon said. The soldier looked at the diplomat nearest to me, who shrugged.

That was a doubtful enough response that the soldier felt he could make the decision. He took aim and fired. The gunshot startled the nearby birds, and the bullet bounced harmlessly off Zephyr's torso.

The diplomats gasped, and the soldier lowered his weapon.

"I don't want to threaten you, nor do I want to force you to let me use the portal. If I'm right about the threat this dark elf poses, you need us." I added, "I won't ask for anything else. I just want to locate the artifact, same as I've wanted the whole time I've been here."

"Okay," Mr. Jansen said. "But I'm under orders to stay with you. I'm coming as well, and the soldiers will also be with us. I think my colleagues should remain on this side."

"I can live with that."

There were nods, and I exhaled in relief. It looked like we were going through yet another open portal. We needed to find a way to close them all.

CHAPTER FOURTEEN

The portal was the smallest I'd seen so far and also the most beautiful. It was surrounded and protected by ornately carved stone. The carvings were worn, and I didn't think they were runes, but this place had been loved.

I could feel its power. The portal shimmered as the others did. What was most impressive was the lack of pillars or signs that there had been any.

This portal had either never been shut, or someone had opened it a long time ago and taken great pains to remove any signs that it had been closed. If the latter was true, it was likely done at the same time someone had made the surround. From the feel of the rock, that hadn't been in the last thousand years.

I hadn't expected to see another portal during my search for an artifact.

"Has anyone been through it?" Zephyr asked as everyone entered the small room around it.

"Not that we're aware of," Mr. Jansen replied. "We have

not authorized travel through it. Our government wanted to know it was safe on the other side before anyone went through. Our scientists have been studying it."

No sooner had he said this than two people appeared, a man and a woman, through a door at the back of the room. One carried a clipboard and the other a scanner. They stopped when they saw us.

"Aella Carter?" the woman asked. "Are you Aella Carter?"

"Yup," I replied. She looked from me to Zephyr and then at Roth, Sen, and Nuri, the latter two riding on my shoulders.

"I can't believe it. You're here. *You're here.* I've wanted to meet you for so long. Did they call you in to assess the portal for us and work out if it is safe?"

I lifted an eyebrow, but Jansen beat me to giving the negative.

"This is the person you've been requesting to assist us?" the guy asked, his accent thicker and his words harder to understand.

"Yes. She's the most powerful elf on the planet and the only one to use all four elements. She's also traveled through the portals mentally and physically."

"Mentally?" Mr. Jansen asked.

I nodded and explained that I could reach through using the elements, then described how that was done. While the two scientists understood, the rest of the contingent didn't.

I moved closer to the portal and reached toward it. It greedily sucked me in, then pulled my mind across. It stretched me but more gently than the other portals.

This portal was different. Traveling through it was easier, more...natural. I didn't feel the tug on my mind or resources like I had with the others. It was liberating.

My mind popped out on the other side, but I paused, my body on one side and my mind on the other.

It's okay. I've got you, Zephyr assured me. I felt as if he'd hugged me from the other side of the portal.

Focusing on what we needed to do, I reached for the elements around the portal to get an idea of what was waiting. What I found surprised me. Other than a very small crack that didn't allow natural air to come through, there was nothing but a box around the portal.

Although it took me a moment, I realized that someone had buried the portal on the other end. It was below the surface.

I spread my control out farther to find the artifacts I sought, but there was nothing but ruined buildings under the soil in a large area. I was sure the buildings had deliberately been buried. The dark elves were not easy to hide from.

The lack of heat in the room also worried me. This wasn't a mission where I could afford to linger on the other side. It didn't have much fresh air, and it was also cold and inhospitable in other ways. I had little choice, however. I needed that artifact I'd come for, and it was through the portal.

As soon as I was satisfied that we'd last long enough to power up my abilities, I pulled back to the room my body was in. We had made progress toward finding our answers, but the biggest change was a long desk laid out nearby. It had several human-created devices on it.

I wasn't sure what they were for, but I thought I recognized some of them as devices Minsheng used when we were studying the portal and other elemental-related things. They were for the scientists.

Zephyr still had his arm around my waist, and there were still many diplomats in the room. I told them what I'd felt on the other side and that there was very little space or air. That caused concern until I pointed out that I could widen the airways and tunnel out.

Of course, I didn't plan to go any farther than the artifact I needed, but it would be a start. It would allow them to explore the other side in relative safety.

I did my best not to get frustrated when the diplomats then insisted they make a plan, tweak it, and debate every detail, then focused on telling some higher authority they had done so.

"I don't have time for any more delays," I said when my patience ran out. "There are three other portals, and the elves who are guarding them are in danger every moment I am away from them. I need to find that artifact and return it to them."

"You can't go through that portal alone. We won't allow it," Jansen replied, folding his arms.

I had to fight not to roll my eyes, but I couldn't start an international incident because they didn't understand how weak their negotiating position was.

"Then you can come with me," I shot back. "Just try not to breathe much until I get the air supply sorted."

I didn't give them a chance to object, just moved toward the portal again, Zephyr and Roth came close, and Nuri and Sen sat on my shoulders. Thankfully, Jansen didn't argue, just hurried over to stand with us.

"Right. You shouldn't feel any pain, but it's weird going over. Takes longer than you think it will, and you feel whole and not whole at the same time. You'll come out the other side at the same speed you went in, like stepping off the end of a travelator. Got it?"

"I think I can handle that."

"Great. I'll go first with Nuri and Sen. Then you can come through with Roth, and Zephyr will bring up the rear."

Once again, I didn't wait for anyone to object. This was my mission, and I was bringing him along to keep the country I was in happy. I didn't want to be forced to take orders or prevented from doing what was required.

I stepped through the portal, marveling at how easy it felt. I was getting used to how strange the journey felt and having my mythicals with me but not being able to sense them. I knew I had a body but couldn't flex my fingers or exhale. It also took a long time, longer than normal, which made me worry.

I stepped out on the other side. The room I was in was so dark I could barely make out Nuri and Sen. Instead of using my eyes, I reached out with my mind and felt for the earth and stone around me. I took a couple of tentative steps away from the portal to make room for Roth, Jansen, and Zephyr.

After I did that, Roth and Jansen came through, the latter gasping and stumbling. Roth caught him, and I reached out to steady him and draw him away from the portal.

"It's so dark," he exclaimed.

"Not too loud," I replied, barely above a whisper. "We might be in a building, but I've always found it wise not to draw attention to myself while I was on this planet."

It wasn't true, but Jansen didn't say another word and let me focus again. I connected with the nearest elements and felt along the crack to where a small amount of air was circulating. I widened it, making it smooth and a good shape for air to blow from above.

The interior was colder than I'd expected, and I started shivering and wishing I'd brought a jacket with me. This was less than ideal. Nuri flew off my shoulder as Zephyr appeared, his mind reaching out to merge with mine.

Instead of helping me get air into the room, Zephyr made a perch partway up one of the walls, and Nuri landed on it before turning into a fireball.

I grinned as the small room was flooded with light. The flickering flames showed the room as it had been for thousands of years, the beautiful carvings on the stone walls being seen for the first time in that long. As on the other side, there was a stone arch over the portal that framed it and acted as protection.

The light also showed the frost that had crept into the edges of the room. Wherever we were, it was cold.

I continued to think of a way we could warm the room. Nuri could produce some heat, and I didn't doubt he could make the room warmer, but it was going to take a long time.

"We can't stay like this. We're going to get hypothermia," Mr. Jansen said, looking at me as if I were mad and blowing on his fingers. I didn't respond, just worked with Zephyr on widening the small route to the surface.

It was even colder as we got nearer the surface, and my mind connected with snow. This was only a temporary solution to the air problem.

"Go back to the other side and ask them to get us coats and some flashlights. We need to make this work, or we'll suffocate before you get back."

Jansen's mouth opened as he thought of something to say. In the end, he walked back into the portal, leaving me in peace with my mythicals.

We worked fast, getting a funnel open and clearing the snow from above it, so it had an open run from the outside world to here. Although it would replenish the air eventually, I was sure the air in here was much lower on oxygen than normal, so I took control of it and quickly cycled it in and out.

Before long, it was easier to breathe and warmer. Zephyr and I added heat once we weren't as focused on the outside and making sure we didn't suffocate.

By the time Jansen came back with several coats, we were exploring the area to find the artifact we needed.

I frowned when I searched as far out as I could and still didn't detect anything. It had to be here somewhere. I hadn't come all this way to find nothing.

"It's warmer in here," Jansen said, smiling as he held out a coat to me.

I smiled back, but I wasn't sure I didn't grimace. There was a strange irony to all this. I kept closing portals and protecting humanity, and the universe kept showing me more open portals and a desire to explore and get into trouble that even I wasn't sure I could sway.

If we can get the Texas portal closed, maybe we can make a difference, Zephyr reminded me. I wasn't sure he believed it anymore either.

I didn't have time to dwell on doubts. I had to keep going and hope for the best. My people needed me; they were counting on me to deliver. I couldn't come back empty-handed.

Zephyr and I moved toward what must have once been an entry. The door was still there, intact and as beautiful as the stonework around it with carved elves and a garden on it, but it was shut now, and the hallway beyond was full of dirt. It felt like it had been deliberately filled in, much like the building around the portal in California.

We used our powers to work the earth out of the way since that was the path of least resistance, the route out of here that made sense. I was nervous. This was taking a lot of energy, and I still couldn't feel an artifact anywhere in the area.

Still, we pushed on, moving enough dirt that the door could swing open. Once we could see the hall, our task grew simpler, and the pair of us worked to move it as we stepped closer to the surface.

"Wow," Jansen said when we'd moved through far enough that he could come up behind and see what we were doing. "You can dig us out of here, can't you?"

"Hopefully. I can't figure out how far it goes. I'll open up what I can, and you can explore it more and figure out its uses once we're gone. I'm trying to get to the artifact we need without drawing attention from any dark elves near-by," I replied.

It was a blunt statement, and I said it with enough conviction that Jansen didn't speak again, just let us get on with it.

CHAPTER FIFTEEN

Three hours later, I was hungry again, and my feet were killing me. I was sure I had blisters, and I was grumpier than ever. This wasn't what I'd imagined when I'd set out on this quest.

On top of being cooped up in an old, buried city, I was aware of how long we'd been away from our friends and how drained my elemental magic was. We couldn't keep this up much longer before we were going to have to abandon our plan.

I tried not to let worry drag down my mood, but I was growing more irritable. The situation reminded me of being stuck in the cult mountain the first time, moving around in the dark and using our earth abilities to get out. That felt like a lifetime ago now.

Stopping again, I closed my eyes and reached for an artifact or an elemental power source. The portal continued to be a beacon of elemental magic, and it was hard to ignore its tug; I needed something smaller and more subtle than that.

There, Zephyr said, moving our focus off to one side and out of the way.

I wasn't sure where he meant, but then I picked up on the faint pull of something fire-based. Was that the artifact we had come to find?

There was no way to know until we got closer, so we did not waste time. We hurried that way, our hands entwined and everyone trailing after us.

Every little while, we made Nuri another perch, and the firebird lighted the way for us. I could tell Sen and Roth were bored and struggling. It wasn't easy to be cooped up in stone and earth.

I was sure Jansen was tired as well, but he amused himself by taking photos of the carvings and the items we uncovered. There were a surprising number of tools and everyday items preserved in the near-frozen earth.

Now that we had something to aim for, we cleared the corridors in that direction, uncovering more rooms in the same building. It appeared to be a massive dwelling, with rooms that branched in multiple directions from the main hub.

Although it must have been an interesting place to live, I had to constantly reach ahead to make sure I was still on the correct route. We had reached a warmer area as well, so the need for Nuri to be a fireball lessened.

He returned to normal. Jansen held a flashlight for us to make himself useful.

Puzzled by the greater heat, I reached out to the air and found that some of the building was open, not buried.

I paused, concerned. That wasn't what I'd expected.

The artifact is being used, and it's in an occupied dwelling, Zephyr said, confirming my fears.

Can we take it, then?

If dark elves are using it, why not?

I shuddered at the coldness in the statement and the thought. Could we be that callous? Could we take something that was keeping others alive?

We couldn't be sure unless we tried since we had no information. We needed to find out who was using the artifact without drawing attention to the portal.

After letting Jansen know what we'd found, we pushed on via a route that got us close to the artifact before we uncovered it. It meant wiggling around, but it couldn't be helped.

Sure we were going to need extra power before we were done with our mission, I retrieved the helmet. I put it on and tapped the crystals for the power I needed to move the air and earth.

The next section of the building was easy to clear. Minutes later, we were standing about fifty feet from the artifact. It was on the other side of a wall in the uncleared corridor. It wouldn't take much to clear the next section, so we paused, reaching to the elements on the other side.

Our minds brushed against another's, which was controlling the air on the other side. I pulled back, frowning. This was not a complication I'd foreseen. When we'd been sent to find this artifact, we'd believed it to be on Earth in a place we'd be able to search.

Now I was hiding from other elves, with no idea if they were friend or foe, and I was drained of elemental magic.

Jansen didn't say anything, letting Zephyr and me figure out what to do.

I think we should push through and make sure whoever it is can't run or yell for help, Zephyr said. *If they're a dark elf, kill them, and if not, offer to bring them and any elves with them back with us to the Sanctuary. They're squatting here. They might want to meet the descendants of the elves who made it.*

My dragon had a good point, and it made my mind up. It was time to act and finish this mission once and for all. We redirected the rest of the dirt and removed the barrier between us and whoever was on the other side.

"Stay back," I told Jansen as we broke through and light became visible.

As soon as I could see an elf on the other side—a teenage lad who was on his feet, his mouth open as he stared at us—I took control of the air and made barriers that would keep him and any sounds we made inside.

"Hi," I began when I'd finished. "We mean no harm."

The teenager looked at us, his eyes widening as he took in the mythicals.

"Are there others here we can talk to?" I asked, taking a slow step closer. "We're from Earth. If you're hiding from the dark elf, we can help."

It was a huge risk to say that, but I had to take it. I'd found that bringing the dark elf into a conversation swiftly showed where the allegiance of a new elf lay.

"My family is here, and some friends. We've been hiding for several weeks, but the dark elf patrols are getting closer. They know we're here, but they don't like to come deep into the old city," the kid replied.

"Great. Can you summon your family and friends?

We'll get you all out of here and to where they can never find you. The people who made this city went to Earth. We can take you there."

The stunned boy didn't move, and Jansen chose that moment to take my arm to get my attention.

"Are you sure you should offer them that?" he asked. "We don't want to draw the attention of the dark elves, do we? The people who built this city aren't on the other side anymore."

"The people who built this city sent me here," I replied. "They built another in the US. That's how I knew to come here."

Jansen jutted out his jaw as if he were contemplating telling me what he thought about that, but he just gave me a quick nod and let go of my arm.

By the time I turned back to the teenager, he had backed up to a makeshift bed near the bottom of a statue. The statue was holding a small oval stone that was glowing a pale orange and giving off heat.

"Did you activate this?" I asked. It was using the fire elemental, but I was not sure it could be used by anyone.

"No, my mother. We found it here. She said she was drawn to it. It is heating the room and keeping us from dying. We thank the Henera for finding it."

I tried not to react to hearing the title the elves used for me and focused on the problem instead. I couldn't take something these elves needed without making sure they were all safe. Otherwise, I was no better than the dark elf, who took what he wanted without remorse.

I reached for the family of the newly discovered elf and felt movement in the air, as well as the minds of other elves. They were not far away, holding a position. I could feel their control and what they were doing.

I told Jansen and the kid to stay put and rushed off with my mythicals to help. Weaving through the corridors, I followed what I felt until I reached five elves hiding in doorways as they used elemental magic to defend themselves.

I didn't say a word, just stepped into the hall with Zephyr. I'd formed an air barrier in front of us, and our minds reached to control everything the dark elves did.

Everyone reacted to my presence with surprise and the battle stopped for a second, which gave me a chance to wrest control from the dark elves. There were six of them. They weren't armored like others we'd seen, but they were working well together. It took Zephyr and me a moment to push them out.

They recovered quickly, and I blasted air at them. Roth, Nuri, and Sen charged. The myconid knocked two of them out with darts.

I focused on the rest, pinning them with air as Roth blasted them with icy water and Nuri turned into a fireball once more. The elves on our side of the battle took longer to recover. They stared at me for seconds before joining in again, then plants grew and grabbed a leg, yanking it out from under one of the dark elves.

Zephyr used his dagger to whip up more plants and pin another enemy so Sen could shoot him, then they moved on. I was advancing through the tunnel when two more dark elves appeared, coming from the ends of a T junction. I gritted my teeth as I spotted their armor and felt the crystals attached to them. These two were powerful.

Although I wouldn't have worried about taking them on when I was at full strength, I'd pushed myself for the last seven hours, and there wasn't a lot left in my tank. I couldn't let these dark elves get away, however. They'd seen me, so they had to die. All of them.

As I kept the air barrier in place and held the elements around me and the elves I was protecting, I thought of a strategy. Their armor made it hard to use elemental magic to attack them, which meant I had to find another way around it if I was going to keep this fight swift.

Jansen helped, pulling a gun I hadn't realized he had from a holster under his suit jacket. He fired at the left elf, but he dodged in time. It gave me an idea, however. None of these elves were trained in hand-to-hand combat like I was. They had no reason to be, as far as I could tell.

Pulling the air barrier back to defend everyone else, I strode forward and formed another barrier around myself. As soon as I had the dark elves' attention, I sprinted at the first one, using air to make myself faster. I punched him in the face as Zephyr ran up to aid me.

The female dark elf, who was an air elemental as well, took a swing at me, her arm moving fast. Muscle memory from all my training aided me; I blocked the attack and hit her hard, leaving Zephyr to take on the larger dark elf.

We traded blows, our limbs blurring as we struck and blocked and struck again. I tried not to think, just reacted and let my body do what felt right.

She left an opening and I hit her hard in the chest, knocking her back. She smacked her head on the wall behind and went limp. Sen came up and shot her with a dart, putting her out for a while.

I turned again, attacking the final elf from behind and delivering a blow to the neck that sent him to his knees. Zephyr shot a knee into the dark elf's face with a sickening crunch and finished the job, and the attacker reeled back.

There was no need for more darts. Silence fell inside the ruined city.

I exhaled as I looked at the dead or unconscious elves. We had done it; we had not let any of them flee.

We should check that there aren't any others, Zephyr said, his mind reaching through the tunnels around us and taking my merged control with it.

I didn't fight what he was attempting, but I didn't aid him as the other elves recovered from the shock of being rescued. As I pulled the armor off the female dark elf, they emerged from the side tunnels and came closer.

"We mean you no harm," I told them when they hesitated.

As we mentally checked for the presence of more elves, I explained everything to the small group, including where we'd come from and that I needed the artifact but could take them somewhere safer.

There was no hesitation from any of them. They wanted to be safe.

"Do I need to remind you that others will come looking for these dark elves?" Jansen blurted, pale and shaking as he looked anywhere but at the bodies of the dark elves.

"That's simple to solve," I replied. "We make it look as if these elves killed them and fled somewhere else."

I didn't wait for Jansen to react or object but picked up the bodies of the dark elves with my air magic and wafted them through the tunnels after us. It was important to make it look as if the family had fled, so we left a bedroll and bloodied clothing from the dark elf who had been shot and made it look as if there had been a fight. Then I made it look like an earth elf had buried the rest of them and fled, leaving them trapped and unable to breathe.

Finally, I filled an open section with dirt and buried the dark elves. Two weren't dead, and I wasn't sure what to do with them, but I couldn't kill them, even if that kept our ruse from being effective.

I opted to bring them back to Earth with us and hold them prisoner. When we were satisfied, I took the artifact, resealed enough of the tunnels to hide where we'd come from, and made my way back to the portal with our new guests.

It wasn't the mission I'd expected, but we'd done it. We'd got the artifact, and we had rescued more elves along the way.

CHAPTER SIXTEEN

As I stood in front of the Texas portal, I realized how much bigger it was than the others we'd seen. I was starting to understand why this one was so important and had been the focus of Kirdash's attention on so many occasions.

Simon and Minsheng came into the room a short while later. Several elves followed them, floating the four pillars we needed. Anyone not necessary for defense had been evacuated from the area and was at a safe distance.

Cherisse, Seth, Orthelo, and Vestan were not far behind since the four of them intended to close the portal. Besides Zephyr and me, they were the four most powerful elves in their elements. Each was more skilled at their element than I was. They focused on one and could be precise.

My job was the same as it had been before: to fill the crystals and ensure they were safely transferred to the pillars. Four large pillars had been created for this portal, and they would be the first things to go into place, each ready for its crystal. An elf of each element was by their pillar, Emily and Erlan having hand-picked the other two from warehouse elves we'd taken in over the years.

Minsheng and the elves were wearing the elemental armor that we'd taken off dark elves in the attacks we had endured and the fights we'd been in on the other side of the portals. It wasn't a perfect plan to keep us safe, but it would be safer than our last attempt at closing and locking a portal had been.

I moved to Simon and Minsheng. My Shishou had made sure that everything was far safer this time with the most volatile part of our mission.

"I've double-checked the connections," Simon told us. "And everything else. It should work this time."

"It better. I'm not taking any more artifacts from people who need them," I replied, noticing he'd repaired the device that channeled elemental energy into the crystals.

"Okay," I said loud enough for everyone to hear. "Let's get this started."

So the elves closing the portal didn't have to wait or hold it shut as long, I put one hand on the device and the other on the connector.

"I'm sure they all have enough power left to get the crystals to the right level," Minsheng added, but I'd begun drawing the energy through me.

It was strange being a conduit for so much elemental energy, but Zephyr's mind was merged with mine, and it went a lot smoother and more gently than the last time we'd tried this.

Although I wasn't sure how long it would take to make the transfer, I kept my cool and let it happen. Behind me, I could see the four elemental elves wrestling with the portal, getting it to let them begin the unraveling process.

My mind wasn't merged with theirs this time, so each was holding a rune-covered tablet to get the boost they needed. I had my helmet by my feet in case I needed it, but the four of them would have benefitted from it more. The strain on their faces was evident, and it made me wonder how the portals had been shut the first time.

Think we should help them? Zephyr asked.

I frowned, then gave him the go-ahead. We needed to get this portal closed, and I didn't want to wait around with full crystals in a volatile state while they shut it.

Before Zephyr could reach out to begin merging us with them, a dark elf came through the portal, followed by another and another.

Shitsticks, Zephyr, Roth, Sen, Nuri, and I all thought.

"Attack," Cherisse yelled as one of the dark elves air blasted the four closing the portal out of the way.

I snatched control of the air before it could hit them and spread it out, so they were only hit with a gust of wind that blew back their hair and clothing.

"Simon, make a barrier over the portal opening," I commanded. "And get more elves in here."

Minsheng ran off to do the last part, calling for backup as soon as he had the door open.

More dark elves appeared, but Simon was a proficient air elf, and he blasted the majority back through the portal. I had no idea if the elves trying to shut the portal could do so while the dark elves were traveling through it, but we had to try. If the dark elves died in transit, so be it.

Zephyr and I continued to merge our control with the

four elves and lend them strength, but I could feel their problem. Kirdash was there, holding onto the other end of the portal.

I swore. I was forced to slow the transfer of energy from the artifacts to the crystals while I helped keep the portal from being overwhelmed. Of all the times to begin an attack, Kirdash had chosen to do so as we started to close it. Nothing we did was ever simple.

It took all my concentration to push against Kirdash with my fellow elves and manage the transfer, Zephyr concentrating hard as he did the same. Not much later, the elves from the pillars joined us, merging their minds and lending us another boost of power. That left Simon defending us.

Roth, Nuri, and Sen rushed into the center, along with the mythicals the elves had bonded with. Roth head-butted one of the dark elves back into the portal as Sen bounded up and hit another with a dart. Nuri went full fireball and flew into the face of another. The dark elf staggered back as a vine grew behind him, then he tumbled back through the portal.

"Barrier in place for now," Simon yelled as he stepped closer.

It didn't take long for the barrier to become visible, the air elf pulling the warmer air away from the cool and packing it so densely it froze the moisture in the air.

The next few dark elves who came through bounced off it and fell back into the portal. If Kirdash's mind hadn't been reaching through the portal, pushing against our control, we'd have been able to hold, but as it was, we needed help.

Thankfully, Minsheng chose that moment to return. He had every elf on the base with him.

"Half the air elves merge with Simon and hold the barrier," I ordered. "The rest merge with Cherisse, Seth, Orthelo, and Vestan. The dark elf wants to test our strength. Let's show him what we're made of."

There was a chorus of battle cries, yells of "Henera," and growls of anger at the surprise attack. Then elves merged their minds with ours, making us even more powerful. Although they were of decent strength, we had the three strongest on the planet working together, so I was surprised to find that it made so much difference.

Kirdash held firm, and I worried as more dark elves came through, growing warier as time passed. The ones coming knew the state of the cavern and what they needed to do.

Pushing back the dark elves got slower, and I could see Simon grimacing despite the help he had. I reached for the helmet with my mind, using my air power to lift it while my hands remained locked in place, charging the crystals. If we didn't stop this attack, the crystals being charged wasn't going to matter.

As soon as the helmet was on, I connected to it. I started draining the crystals, boosting the defenders I was merged with. I added my mind to Simon's as well, now linked directly or indirectly to every element in the room and the portal.

The strain as I acted as a conduit for the power exchange was so much an ache grew in my head and my body shook, but I didn't stop, instead diverting a small amount of power from the artifacts.

While Kirdash held onto the portal, he focused the majority of his energy on attacking Simon and taking control of the barrier the elf scientist had created across the portal.

Simon sank to his knees, gritting his teeth against the pain when Kirdash latched onto his mind as he'd done with me and my bonded mythicals.

I attacked the grip the way I did when I was the target, coming in from the side and breaking his hold bit by bit. I could see the relief on Simon's face. He looked my way as Nuri flew back to me, becoming a normal bird as he landed on my shoulder and helped guide my mind.

I didn't know what I'd have done without the experienced firebird as I fought Kirdash's grip. My attacks drew his ire, and he switched targets as Simon got to his feet. Pain flared in my head as Kirdash pushed against my mind so hard I reeled and almost lost my grip on the artifacts and the device.

My mind and control were pulled in many directions by the elves I was merged with, so I couldn't fight Kirdash effectively. He was soon in my mind, his grip stretching to my bonds.

Hello again, my dear. My, my, aren't we busy with our friends.

I tried not to respond, not wanting Kirdash in my head but not sure how to get him out when I was so strained. It took all my concentration to keep him from attacking my bonds, and I drew elemental energy from the artifacts as Kirdash pushed.

Focus, Henera, Nuri cautioned. *Close eyes and calm emotions, then fight as you know how. Kirdash has never won against you. You think him strong, but you are far stronger. He hides like coward, attacking when you're distracted and busy. Follow your instincts.*

His words calmed me and I focused, knowing it was better to draw the power I needed and not charge the crystals than to focus on charging the crystals when we hadn't pushed Kirdash back yet.

I lashed out, hitting the merged connections and my bonds as hard as I could. It wasn't easy to hold everything together and help Simon with his barrier, plus assist the four elves holding the portal shut it and protect and defend against elemental attacks from the dark elves who had made it through the gate.

There was almost no progress as more dark elves appeared and skirted the edge of the barrier. It was solid and kept a lot of us safe, but it was so cold that it was visible.

Bit by bit, I pushed Kirdash back mentally. My physical body remained connected to the artifacts and crystals. I also drew from the helmet, and it made me marvel at how much elemental energy I could channel and use. Over the last few years, I had become so powerful that I could handle far more elemental energy than almost the rest of the elves in the room combined.

I wielded it now, pushing back Kirdash's control and strengthening and making Simon's barrier larger until the dark elves were penned in with nowhere to go. That gave our elves a reprieve, and they used it to turn their efforts to fighting Kirdash for control of the portal.

With the renewed effort from all of us, we made

progress, and the dark elves were pushed back into the portal. Kirdash continued to fight, however.

Although we had to keep him at bay, I returned my focus to charging the crystals and let Zephyr fight the dark elf and push him back.

"The crystals are almost full," Simon said. "We'll need to move them soon."

I gulped, knowing the others weren't ready.

"Get them in the pillars anyway," Vestan called. "We'll get the portal partially shut."

I wanted to object, but calm came from Nuri, with a projected image of elves doing something very similar I'd seen in drawings. It was a memory from the previous time the portal had been closed, when the great elves had fought Kirdash in much the same way we were. It explained why the portal hadn't quite been closed and minds could still connect across it—Kirdash had held the mental component open.

"Keep going," I agreed.

Everyone did, and Zephyr and the others finally broke the connection, more energy flooding into us as they rapidly worked to unravel the circle of light shimmering in the center of the cavern.

I was relieved that they'd gotten that far, but the energy from the portal physically unlinking had one place to go: into me. I funneled it into the crystals.

"They're ready," Simon declared seconds later. "Get them into the pillars."

Taking my hand off the artifacts, I also disconnected from my helmet and focused on the four crystals. I gently connected them to me, knowing how volatile all four were and wanting to keep them stable. With every mind merged, it tapped the others' energy, but they were also drawing from me.

As long as each mind withdrew before they were so worn out they couldn't keep going, we wouldn't have any trouble. I picked up the crystals with my mind, then floated them toward their pillars and the holes in the top. I walked closer as I did, encouraging everyone except the elementals at each pillar to get out of the area the forcefield would be created in.

The portal was unwinding slowly, but I tried not to worry about how long it was taking. Kirdash was still fighting it. Zephyr kept pushing him back, however, forcing him to relinquish control.

I took steady breaths and steady steps. Nuri settled on my shoulder again, sending waves of calm and comfort my way.

We moved the crystals closer, each receiving elf preparing the runes in the pillars to adhere to what would power them. It was like two halves of a connection coming together, each one volatile and needing coaxing until they were close enough to reach out and realize they needed each other.

The moment they were connected, the field would activate, but they were in a careful balance. All four needed to be activated at the same moment so the pillars recognized each other as part of the same forcefield and powered device and didn't tear each other apart.

I felt the weight of getting this right, as well as tugs on my abilities in every other direction. My head was pounding, and I couldn't last much longer. This needed to be done and soon.

Kirdash continued to fight, showing he still had energy coming in from somewhere even if he also used power sources to keep going. Finally, the crystals were a half-inch from their final resting places. I could feel the pillars wanting to connect, the powered-up runes yearning to be set loose.

"Connecting now," I called, my voice steady and calm even though I was nervous.

Nuri stayed on my shoulder despite the danger, continuing to work with me as I moved the four crystals the last fraction and connected them. The pillars activated, but Zephyr was prepared. He pulled us out of the forcefield before the pillars could tear us apart.

I exhaled, now safely on the other side of the field with the rest. The problem was, the portal was not shut. It wasn't even as close as it had been last time. I could feel a pulsating spiderweb of light. A mind could still travel between the two worlds.

An elf would be torn apart by the pillars or have to expend an astronomical amount of elemental energy to walk through the forcefield, which meant someone like Kirdash or Zephyr or I could still go through it. The right combination of elemental elves might be able to as well.

It probably meant we didn't have to worry about a full-force attack. Kirdash couldn't take on the entire planet of elves alone. That, I was certain of.

For now, we needed to rest.

CHAPTER SEVENTEEN

There was nothing left to say as Minsheng finished reporting what had happened at the Texas site to the officials on the screen. I had kept quiet for most of the conversation. I'd not slept much since our attack, though I'd eaten. My helmet was almost depleted, and several of the artifacts felt a lot less powerful.

I felt guilty for using up the world's most powerful objects to block portals we shouldn't have opened in the first place, but there wasn't a lot to be done about it. I was starting to tire of hiding from Kirdash. Did we have no other options?

Fighting him won't be easy, Zephyr said.

Nothing ever is. We've always run from him or avoided him, and it never goes according to plan. People die and things break, and we survive. At some point, it has to end. It can't be impossible to beat him. I refuse to believe it. Otherwise, he'd walk through a portal and kill us all.

Kirdash is scared, Nuri said, confirming that he believed what we did.

The prophecy does talk about the Henera winning, Roth added. The pegasus was sitting in a large tub of water at the back of the room.

I'm tired of running. I have been for a while, but we're not ready to fight him either. Zephyr gave my hand a squeeze.

Then I guess we'll have to get ready.

"Aella, you there?" the general asked to get my attention. Everyone was staring at me.

"Sorry. I was talking to the others."

"The President asked when you could begin closing the other portals?" The general smiled as he spoke, but it didn't reach his eyes. I was sure that no one was impressed that I hadn't been paying attention.

"We can't," I replied, knowing I was about to piss them off even more. "The artifacts don't have enough power left in them. Kirdash is going to be looking for us to unbury them and attempt to close them. He'll have those portals closely monitored. There's nothing we can do but keep them buried for now."

There was silence after I finished speaking.

"I want to take Kirdash on. It's the only way. Beat him once and for all. Otherwise, we're always going to be dreading the moment he attacks."

"What do you need?" the President asked, the first to acknowledge what I'd said. His voice was quiet but steady. He knew that wasn't a lighthearted statement, that I meant it.

"Anything that can help that we don't have. I want every artifact we know. Instead of using them to shut portals, I want them on all of us who are willing to fight. I want every piece of information known to anyone about what

Kirdash may or may not be able to do. If he can do it, I should be able to as well."

"The Sanctuary has a small list of artifacts and has been working with the organization and Amcika," Sierrathen told everyone. "We'll make sure you get everything we know about, and we'll begin finding you everything we can on the dark elf. I have a feeling the two with the most information are there with you, however."

Everyone looked at Zephyr, Nuri, or both of them when Sierrathen finished speaking. They were the two with memories of the dark elf and the previous battles against him.

I exhaled. I was not sure it would be enough. While they remembered some information, so much time had passed that it was incomplete. It was as good as what they'd known in the first place. Nuri was wonderful at helping me protect against the mental attacks of Kirdash. Zephyr was phenomenal in battle as a dragon and an elementalist because those were the roles their memories reinforced.

What I needed was everything they *didn't* know. That wasn't going to be easy to discover.

We know he heals, Zephyr pointed out. *I know you've begun healing others, but you've never attempted to heal yourself.*

It was a good point. The dark elf had lived for this long because he could heal his body and fix any problem. While I wasn't sure I wanted to live forever, healing in battle was a useful ability. I'd done so once instinctively.

Possibly more than once. When was the last time you remember being hurt for more than a few minutes? Zephyr asked.

I didn't have to think about it for long. I had no memories in the last couple of years of being hurt and not getting better quickly, not since before I'd developed my third element. I'd never been sick, had food poisoning, or anything like that, either.

Was I keeping my body healthy by default?

I kept an air barrier around myself from the moment I woke to the moment I slept, so there was a good chance I was, but it was still a strange thought and one I didn't intend to voice aloud.

Various people spoke up and suggested we use the artifacts to close the portals in case I didn't succeed against Kirdash, but the President stopped the conversation after a moment.

"Although I've been told that I'm the leader of the free world on more occasions than I dare count, I'm sure the power I command no longer holds much weight compared to the number of elves and mythicals who are behind Aella and her bonded companions. If she says she believes the right thing is to fight this dark elf when she has tried several other options, so be it."

There was another silence, and my emotions made my throat close. That wasn't what I'd expected him to say. I *had* expected everyone to object.

"I don't want to force anyone to do anything," I said a moment later. "I never have. I do know we will need as much help as we can get. Using our resources to shut more portals when there are two we don't control and he'll fight us every step of the way doesn't seem wise to me. He's scared to come here. He's afraid. Of us."

This boosted them, and I took a back seat again as they made plans to help me. They asked questions now and then, but mostly, they were willing to work out what could be done among themselves.

When I yawned, they realized we needed to stop and let everyone rest.

The President cut through everything. "I have one last question. This dragon you found with his portal. Is he safe? Does he know anything that can help?"

I sighed, thinking of the frosty reception we'd received. The dragon hadn't liked Zephyr or me much.

"I'll go see him," I replied. "As long as I can sleep on the plane."

Several of the people around me grinned, but it was approved, and I was offered a plane ride immediately. The plane we had used was kept near me these days, and it was ready to go.

With my propensity to keep my go-bag ready, I was heading to the plane in less than half an hour.

Despite my declaration of wanting to take Kirdash on, it was a lot to ask, and it could easily go wrong. On top of that, I was tired and low on elemental energy. Right now, he could probably kill me in minutes.

We don't have to fight him until we're ready, Zephyr remarked.

Although I hoped Zephyr was right, it wasn't always that simple in war. Kirdash might not wait to bring the fight to us. He might not be scared like Nuri thought. There was no way to be sure of anything except that we needed to prepare, and we needed more information. Both required time and hard work.

When I woke up in the back of the plane, we were half an hour from our destination, and there was a meal waiting for me. I ate as we landed, hoping once again that the portals in the US would be safe until I returned.

It was mid-afternoon when we touched down. The time zones and our sleeping patterns were messing with my head enough that it took me a moment to work it out. That meant the Irish farm was busy, and we were spotted long before we arrived.

I waved and looked friendly, but the nearest farmhand didn't even respond before he ran off. I wondered if we were going to be turned away or ignored, but the dragon in human form appeared seconds later from near the barn where the portal was.

"I thought I made it clear that you're not someone I wish to associate with," the dragon growled.

"I'm aware. I wouldn't be here unless I had to be. The choice is yours to make. I'm not here to persuade you of anything. I do need help of an informational kind, however."

I kept my head up as I spoke, meeting the fierce dragon's gaze. He looked at Zephyr, who was in human form, and the other mythicals and seemed to be impressed for a fleeting moment. Before I could be sure, the dragon looked impassive again.

"Very well. Come and ask your questions while I gather the food I need."

Not about to argue with the cranky dragon, I followed him toward the barn, where the farmer and several farmhands were stacking sacks and securing cattle.

"Thank you, my friend," the dragon said as the last of the goods were placed in a pile near the portal.

Although there was a lot of food and animals, I didn't

focus on it. I didn't know what it was for, how many might need feeding, and if this was a regular occurrence.

What did pique my interest was the small pouch the dragon pulled out of his pocket. He opened it to reveal small gemstones, crystals like the ones that powered the artifacts and pillars that protected the portals.

Without thinking, I reached out to them to see if they could be touched. They could, but all of them were empty like they hadn't been activated or hadn't been designed to hold elemental energy. None of them tugged on my mind.

After the farmer inspected them, he nodded and took the pouch. It was a payment, and I politely waited until it was over, not wanting to anger the dragon further.

After the farmer left, the dragon picked up a heavy sack that looked like it contained potatoes and threw it to Zephyr.

"If you're going to demand answers from me, the least you can do is help me get this lot through the portal," he said. He picked up another bag and moved to the portal with it.

They carried the weight to the shimmering circle, and Zephyr followed the dragon's lead as he shoved it through to the other side.

Grinning, I used my elemental abilities to lift the rest of the bags. There had to have been forty of them with grain, fruit, vegetables, and baked goods inside, and I floated them past the dragon and gently through the portal one after the other as he stared.

There were also two cows, three goats, and some sheep. I used air and their leads to guide them to the portal as well.

The livestock was less cooperative, but Zephyr helped me guide them with breezes and nudges until they were all through. Only then did I show any sign of how difficult the task had been, exhaling with relief when the last sheep stepped into the light.

The dragon was still staring at us.

"You know, I could go through that portal now. You've done all my work for me." He folded his arms across his chest.

"Then we'd follow," I replied, folding my arms as well. "Maybe even put it all away for you on the other side."

He smiled, his face breaking into a broad grin that grew wider as the seconds passed.

"I like you more than your ancestors. Come on. I'll put it away while you ask your questions."

Without another word, he went through the portal. After making sure all my mythicals were with me and sending a quick message to the soldiers waiting by the plane to let them know where we were going, we stepped through the portal as well.

It took far less time than normal to arrive out the other side, and I spotted the dragon and everything we'd sent through. A young female elf was herding the animals away, but that was it.

I lifted the rest and made my way after the woman, using the occasional breeze to help her keep the animals on track. We were a long way up a mountain in a full range of giant peaks that ran for miles.

It wasn't that cold despite the altitude, but I wasn't sure why until steam vented out of a hole in the rocks to one side of the path. I jumped, and the dragon laughed.

"Not seen a steam vent from a volcano before?" he asked.

"Not this close, no."

The dragon nodded. "This is an active volcano. It often reminds us why we are so warm up here."

"Active? How do you keep it safe here?"

"We have our ways. An artifact prevents it from being too volatile or unpredictable. Keeps this area safe, but we can't grow much in the way of crops. Not enough moisture."

"Sounds as if you could do with a water elf," I replied.

"You offering?" he shot back.

"Not permanently, but I could come back soon and see what I could do to help or bring one of the other powerful water elves from the Sanctuary. I'm planning on solving your problem in another way first, though."

"You want to take Kirdash on," the dragon stated, taking the wind out of my sails.

"I do. That is why I am here."

"I know nothing of the dark elf, except that he is an abomination and a tyrant and tries to brainwash the other elves by claiming he is Henera. He corrupts innocent minds and enslaves mythicals. Many of the rescued ones never recover. I applaud your courage, but I don't have any secret information to help you."

"You might. Those crystals you gave the farmer...where did you get them? Could they be modified to store elemental energy?"

"I didn't get them anywhere. I make them. They might be able to store elemental energy, but I'd need one that does to know for sure."

I pulled my helmet out of my bag. His eyes went wide, and he held out his hands to take it from me.

"I haven't seen this in a long time. My father made this."

It was my turn to be surprised, but I didn't get long to recover before the dragon thrust it back to me.

"Yes. I can make crystals for items like this. I wouldn't normally be willing to work with an elf who doesn't understand the struggle we face here or one of the arrogant elves who doesn't understand what they're asking, but you've helped without expecting information and offered your energy when it could be spared. You're not like the others. If you help make this place livable in the long term, I will make you all you need in return."

"You have my word," I replied as solemnly as I could.

"Good. If you break it, know that you will have a wrathful dragon to contend with," he threatened, but the corner of his mouth twitched up.

I glanced at him and then Zephyr, trying not to smile. "I know what an angry dragon is like. I try not to get on the wrong side of mine. I give you my word on the bond I share with Zephyr. If I can help another dragon live the life they have chosen for themselves, I will do so."

"Then come. Let us equip you for battle with the dark elf. It's about time someone kicked his ass."

CHAPTER EIGHTEEN

As I stepped off the plane outside the Sanctuary, I couldn't help but smile. I had come back a lot later than I'd originally planned, but it had been worth every moment. Every mythical I was bonded with was sporting one elemental crystal, and I'd put energy in all of them.

With help from two dwarves and a gnome who also lived on the edge of the active volcano, these had then been inset into anklets and a necklace on Roth, a waistband on Sen, and a small jewel that easily attached to Nuri's leg. The helmet was now matching circlets for Zephyr and me, the spare metal being used in the designs for the rest of my mythicals.

They glinted in the sunlight and exuded the elemental magic I'd charged them with, drawing everyone's eyes

Daisy was quick to appear, Sierrathen and Ronan with her. They paused and stared, then Ronan bowed, and the women followed suit. I returned the gesture, making sure I matched the depth.

"The Henera is truly among us," Ronan said as he

straightened. "With every meeting we've had, you are more the woman you were born to be. Today you are every bit her."

I blinked, not sure what to say to such a statement.

"I wasn't sure we could take on the dark elf and win until this moment," Sierrathen began, her expression still reflecting her disbelief. "You continue to surprise me and draw on skills and items that leave the rest of us in the dust."

"If it means we're soon free of the fear the dark elf causes, I don't care what I am or what places I've had to go. On that note, I believe you've given some of your elves the task of fetching artifacts."

"Yes. When we heard you were going to take longer to return, our strongest elves went after the artifacts since they will wield them when the time comes."

"Good. Keep me updated on their progress, and let me know if any elves require assistance. I do not want them to risk their lives unnecessarily. Tell me about the artifacts that were deemed too dangerous for the others."

"There is one in particular," Sierrathen said as we walked through the city toward the kitchens and food hall.

Over the next half-hour, she spoke about an artifact that could be used to boost the range and strength of all the elementals connected to it. It amplified people's natural talent. It had been used in the past to boost a great water elf in a beautiful city as he provided water to the occupants.

I thought about the dragon in the volcanic mountains of the elven homeworld. His life would be improved by such a device. It would perhaps require modification or being combined with another water-based artifact, but given what he was capable of making, I was sure it would solve his problems.

"So, where is it?" I asked Sierrathen, noticing that she had neglected to mention its location.

She didn't respond, her mouth fixed into a line. It didn't bode well.

"It's okay. Wherever it is, I'll find it and bring it back."

"We think it's on the elven homeworld near the dark elf's palace. There's evidence to suggest it was taken there not long after the dark elf started controlling elves and making it hard to control the elements. They saved one of the old cities with it."

"So, what you're saying is, it's right under his nose. Might not even be there anymore, and I will have to go through one of the two buried portals and travel a long way to get there."

"Yes. It could have been left behind. There are other artifacts, but it's the most powerful. With many minds connected to it the way we now know how to do it..."

Sierrathen's voice trailed off. She didn't want to ask me to go get it, but she thought it would be an asset to our fight. Even if it wasn't, it could help the dragon on the other side of the Irish portal. That meant that I had no real choice. I would find it if it still existed.

"I'll go as soon as I've worked out what I'll need to take with me."

"You're not going without me," Daisy told me.

I grinned, not surprised she wanted to come with me. I didn't mind, but I was worried that it was dangerous and pointed that out.

"Everything you do is dangerous. You've said many times that you'd never ask any of us to walk into danger with you, but you go walking into danger for everyone else all the time. I'm coming with you rather than wait at home to patch everyone up."

It was clear she was determined, and help in battle could make a huge difference if used the right way. I planned to take as many with me as wanted to help. Defeating Kirdash and his armies was going to take most of our people.

Of course, retrieving an artifact from under his nose didn't, but I was sure that going alone wouldn't be wise either.

Over the next couple of hours, I made plans and put together a small team. Ronan also insisted on coming and making use of the bow I had been given. Since the Texas portal was safer now, some of the elves there showed an interest. They weren't people I was used to working with or merging my mind with, but I let one of each element come with me.

I asked Cherisse, Vestan, Erlan, and Serfina to come with me. It was a strange mix, but along with Daisy and Ronan and all our mythicals, every elf having a bond, we weren't a small group. The US army insisted on sending along a four-person unit of soldiers headed by the major as well, bringing our number to twenty.

On top of that, we had all the supplies we could want. Every person had a weapon of some kind and enough darts to sink a battleship. We also had all the crystals and arti-facts we owned with us. We weren't going to use them unless we had to so we didn't drain them, but they might be useful.

Finally, we had the invisibility cloaks we'd developed the second time we'd gone through the Californian portal. Nothing would make much difference if the portal was being watched on the other side, but we would cross that bridge when we came to it. I'd do everything I could to keep us hidden.

We boarded the plane and flew to the portal we needed, where we would meet those who came from elsewhere.

When I got there, I didn't let the earth elves unbury the portal right away. I made them wait for me to reach into the earth and feel the area outside the open portal. The tainted elements there showed Kirdash had visited in the past.

No one was controlling them now, however. I grasped them, holding them so I'd know if anyone or their minds came through this gate, and gave the go-ahead for the earth elves to open the way for us.

They were going to make a small tunnel and close it after us. We were going to be gone for a day, maybe two, so it couldn't be left unburied. The last thing they needed was to be attacked while we were on the other side, too far away to rescue them.

With no good form of communication from the other side of the portal, we were going to have to trust that we could return, and so were they. It was similar to our previous adventures on the elven homeworld.

It took over an hour to make a narrow tunnel, but it was finally done. I led the way, a flashlight guiding my path. I continued to hold onto the area around the portal until I was a hundred feet from it. To check if it was safe, I pushed my mind through.

Zephyr slipped his arm around my waist, holding the flashlight and guiding me. My body moved with his as my mind traveled between the planets. It reached the other side, all control and elements as I spied what was there and checked if anyone was watching the portal.

I found two watchers several hundred yards away, sitting behind a sand dune. I didn't feel anyone else, but I warned Zephyr.

Can you knock them out before we go through? Or box them in with a barrier so they can't go anywhere? Zephyr asked.

I thought about it, realizing I couldn't feel the control of either of them. They weren't holding onto any elements. The more I felt around them, noting the movement of the air, the more convinced I became that they were asleep.

When I told Zephyr, he chuckled. I vaguely heard him give everyone the go-ahead to step through the portal. He moved my body through to join my mind, which stopped me from feeling like I had been split in two.

This was going to be a strange experience, and I hoped it worked. Cherisse and Sierrathen had assured me it was possible and it wouldn't do me any harm not to bring my mind back first as I had done on every previous occasion. If it was not fine, I would find out.

Having my body travel while my mind was on the other side of the portal was very odd, but it helped pass the time more swiftly. My mind was occupied with monitoring the sleep patterns of the dark elf guards.

They slumbered as my body and my companions joined me. When my body reached the desert, my mind was sucked back in with a snap and a pop in my head. I blinked as my brain recalibrated to where I was and what I could see.

As soon as I was able, I reached out and checked that the elves were still sleeping.

While everyone was fanning out to defend the area and get their bearings, I created two small boxes of air and suffocated the guards in their sleep. It was the kindest method to get them out of our way, though I felt guilty about it. However, they had chosen to ally with the dark elf, and if they had a chance, they would happily kill us.

I used my magic to bury their bodies, neither of them having armor or anything of value in other ways. They had been the lowest level of guards, and I was relieved. Kirdash was busy elsewhere.

I ushered the others on, but the truth was, this was a large group, and we had a lot of food and supplies with us. We had very little idea about what to expect other than the desert area we'd seen. This wasn't what the whole planet looked like since the portal to the dragon's home was on a mountain.

I hate sand, I said as we set off and began climbing small dunes. *It gets everywhere.*

Me too, but sand with no water is far worse than sand with an ocean beside it. Roth's voice was sad; it reminded me that he was a long way from the place he loved, and we hadn't been back to the coast in a long time. Sen exuded a similar sadness sometimes. This wasn't easy on any of us.

As we trudged along, I thought about all the places I had called home, stayed at temporarily, or visited, and real-ized I'd packed so much into the last few years that I didn't belong anywhere anymore. I'd thought the warehouse in LA was my forever home after we'd finished the renovations. I'd continued to modify it, but it was being neglected right now.

There had been other places too. Thanks to the Amcika cult that had made me and forged my future, I owned a lot of real estate. I had sold some of it along the way to pay for things we all needed, but I'd kept most of it. There were some wonderful places, especially the ranch we'd once fought outside of.

I hoped to go back there, but it wasn't home either. Not yet.

We could live on this planet once Kirdash is dealt with. Zephyr's voice didn't come with an indication of his desire either way, but it was an interesting idea. Could we live here?

I didn't know, but I pondered that as we trekked to the last known whereabouts of the artifact we sought.

CHAPTER NINETEEN

I tried not to let the disappointment show on my face. We'd found the edges of what we thought was the ruined city late the night before. After walking all day and into the night, it had looked like a good place to stop. We'd woken to find it was nothing but small huts that must have marked a village on a road that no longer existed.

I had no idea how much farther we had to go, but we were low on water, and we'd eaten half the food we'd brought with us.

"It should be close by," Ronan said, the one most responsible for navigating where we were going. "Not far."

I wanted to protest that any farther was too far, but I couldn't indulge that part of me. We needed this artifact.

"There's a storm coming." Vestan pointed at the horizon. It was a roiling mess of sand, and I gulped.

Although I'd never been in a sandstorm, I had heard about them, and they were unpleasant. On Earth, they could last for days, and people were killed in them. On top of that, they hurt, the sand blasting the skin and tearing apart bodies that were too frail to withstand them.

This was bad. This was very bad.

I grabbed the air around us and formed a barrier so we'd be safe for a while. Zephyr and Vestan added their minds to mine when they realized what I had done and why. It wasn't an ideal situation, but I thanked whoever was listening that I was an elemental and could protect us this way.

As the sandstorm rolled closer, it parted at the tip of the barrier and rolled around us, blotting out the world in every direction and rising so high I had to keep extending the barrier upward. It threw a constant stream of wind and sand at us.

"Anyone know what direction we need to move in?" I asked a moment later, the whistle of the sand and wind around the barrier loud enough that I had to raise my voice to be heard.

My abilities were being drained by holding the sand out, so I hoped someone had an answer. This was an awful situation to be in when we didn't know where we were or what we were looking for.

Trying not to show the fear and doubt that had crept into my heart, I looked at Ronan. The centaur was standing in the middle of the space I'd created, looking at the sky as if it held the clue. Thanks to the barrier, it was still visible above us.

Finally, he looked at me with a very set expression. "This way. I am not sure, but I am certain enough."

Given no one else had a clue and the soldiers'

compasses didn't work properly on this planet, it was the input we needed.

With help from Zephyr and Vestan, I moved the barrier as we trudged in the direction Ronan led.

We traveled in that way for several hours, not trying to shout over the din. At length, my barrier reached the edge of an object large enough that I couldn't easily move it around it.

Reshaping the barrier and then parting it brought the ruins of a house into the safe zone. I moved toward the structure, which had no roof and broken walls.

It was something to be hopeful about, however. The presence of more dwellings let us know we might be in the right place. I felt more buildings to our right and ahead.

Pointing forward, I encouraged everyone to head that way. Even if it wasn't the city we were looking for, it hopefully had shelter so we could drop the barrier for a while. My abilities were draining, and Vestan was struggling.

I guided us to some relatively intact structures near the center since the dwellings on the edges had largely been worn away by time. It made sense, but I was grateful when we found one with a roof, even if the upper floors were gone and the inside had been overtaken by weeds.

Some appeared to be sound and ended up not being so, holes in the structure letting the wind and sand inside. Eventually, we found a building to protect us, and we all huddled within.

The space was cramped, not large enough for us to all lie down and rest, but we could sit and I could stop using my magic.

"How long do you think it will last?" the major asked.

"We have no way of knowing," Ronan replied.

"They can last a week sometimes," Vestan said.

Before I could ask how he knew, Cherisse beat me to it.

"The refugees we took in have talked of the many challenges they had faced, and I like to listen to their stories of our home planet. One day I hope we can return here in peace. Have portals open and go back and forth. Have two worlds providing for all the races alike."

"I must admit, when I told the wife I was coming here again, she grew jealous. She likes the idea of living on a different planet. Of being one of the first humans to," one of the soldiers piped up.

"If we beat Kirdash, I don't see why not," I replied.

"Do you think you'll get to make that call?" Seth asked. "This is the elven homeworld. It might upset a lot—"

"I don't see why anyone in this room would object to having humans here," I said, cutting him off. "Who sits beside you, risking their lives to protect every race and every living soul on both planets?"

Seth glanced at the soldier beside him. For a second, I worried he was going to dig his heels in since his pride had gotten in the way in the past. I'd had to reprimand him publicly. Eventually, he nodded.

"You're right. Forgive me. We've been in this together for a long time, and I've fought alongside every race. It's no different. We all want to live in peace and protect those we care about."

"It's okay," the soldier said. "Humanity hasn't earned any grace over the course of history, but the majority of us do want exactly that. It's worth making a stand for. Worth fighting to get to the point where no one has to fight anymore."

"And that's worth holding onto. Eat and rest, everyone. I'm going to fly up and see if I can figure out how long this is going to last," I said as I got up.

There were wide eyes, but no one objected to having more information. Zephyr stood as well.

It will tire us less to work together. I'm not letting you fly above this storm alone.

I need you here to guide me back, and we have to preserve our energy. It will be harder on me but use less.

I could feel Zephyr's conflicted feelings. He wanted to argue with me and do what was best for the group.

Feel for the artifact from here first. This is the city we were looking for.

Although I didn't want to delay, he was right. If the artifact was close, we might be able to get it sooner rather than later and make our way out of the storm without waiting for it to pass.

Closing my eyes to block out the presence of the people around me and make it easier to focus, I let my mind merge with Zephyr's. We spread out, feeling for anything we could connect with, but the area around us held only empty houses and ruins.

We weren't in the center of the city, but it wasn't far away. The bigger buildings in the middle were sturdier and more protected and had held up better. If we had not been in a sandstorm, I would have wanted to go exploring. This city had been built when our race was mighty and strong.

Before Kirdash. Before there was strife with humanity. This was from the past, one I wanted to take my race back to. Thinking of humanity joining us in that harmony was motivating. I'd fought with humans, but I'd also grown up among them.

Just like all the races, humanity had a phenomenal capacity for good and evil. It depended on the heart of each individual and if they had the support they needed to recover from past wounds and trauma. If they had meaningful relationships and focused on understanding rather than fear. Fear had a lot to answer for.

Despite reaching as far as we could, I couldn't sense anything. If the artifact was here, it wasn't in the part of the city we were in.

I think there is something right on the edge of our range to the north, Zephyr said. *I can't be sure.*

When I fly, I'll head that way, I replied as we unmerged our minds. I opened my eyes and he smiled at me, his sweet expression warming.

With a nod, I made my way to the door and created a barrier around myself, making my body aerodynamic with some space around me so I could see. Then I powered into the storm.

I concentrated on ascending slowly, tweaking my barrier as I went, so I gained the maximum protection for the least effort. I could feel the tug of my mythicals behind me, Zephyr's absence worse than the others. However, it gave me a solid anchor, and he would keep them safe if anything happened while I was gone.

I had wanted to bring him with me, but the others were in the ruins of a building, and Zephyr had the skill to form a barrier around that many people if the storm blew the roof off or it was otherwise damaged.

This was the sensible course of action, but it didn't keep me from wishing I could take him with me as I ascended through the storm and the distance between us increased.

The buffeting winds were full of sand that made it hard to see, and their howls made it impossible to hear anything else. Of everything I'd expected to face on this mission, this hadn't been it.

Eventually, the sand thinned, more light was visible around me, and the sky took on a glow. The sun had moved toward the horizon as we'd hurried through the storm into the city and rested indoors. I was finally out and above it all.

I could only marvel at the nature around me and the beautiful sky above. I'd not realized I had missed the warmth of the sun until it shone on me. I closed my eyes and just *felt*.

My abilities were drained from getting us to the city, so I didn't indulge for long. I opened my eyes again to look around. It was time to figure this out.

Although I wasn't sure which way the wind was blowing, I started by looking in the direction it had originally come from. I had to rise to spot the edge of the storm, but eventually, I was high enough to see the horizon.

I tried to detect if the sand was moving in any direction, but I couldn't tell. I slowly turned, looking for the edge with the most change to see where it was heading and if it was stronger or weaker in any direction.

As I rotated, dread grew in my heart and made me want to sink. The sandstorm was uniform no matter where I looked. The air was rotating but stationary.

This wasn't natural. This storm was the work of something or someone, and it was centered on us. It wasn't going anywhere.

We're not alone, Zephyr said a second later. *There are elves in this storm with us.*

You're under attack, I replied, dropping back toward the building. I didn't get far before I was hit with a blast of air.

It knocked me north, away from the mythicals and friends I'd left behind.

Seconds later, a group of dark elves rose out of the storm, flying and working together.

"Get out of my way, or you're going to meet your Maker before this fight is done," I called across the sky, funneling my voice toward them to make sure they heard it.

My words were met with laughter as they challenged me for control of the air I was using to fly. I'd remade my air barrier, and I could easily resist their minds; the group was strong but no match for me when I was in my best element.

Another elf rose behind them, however, coming up out of the storm as if he were parting the finest of silks. He wore a stunning array of bright clothing, each item studded with gemstones. On his head was a crown like the circlets Zephyr and I had just acquired, with one exception. This elf's headgear sported several crystals of each color.

I didn't need the elf to reach out and show me what his control felt like for me to know who was in the sky in front of me.

This was Kirdash.

I was face to face with the most powerful elf in two worlds.

CHAPTER TWENTY

"Is it you, my dear?" Kirdash asked.

I gulped and didn't respond.

Get back here, Zephyr screamed, but I couldn't take this dark elf anywhere near my mythicals. While Kirdash was up here with me, the others were safer and had a chance to get away.

Abort the mission. Get everyone back to the portal. I'll catch up.

No, Zephyr yelled.

I gave you an order, I replied. *Get everyone back to the portal and through. We can't fight Kirdash yet. We're not strong enough, and this storm is of their making.*

Zephyr didn't respond, and I wasn't sure he intended to obey me, but I didn't get a chance to say anything else.

As he flew closer to me, Kirdash grinned as if he sensed the argument I was having with Zephyr.

"I didn't think you left your mythicals," Kirdash continued. "It seems you do. Thank you for making my life easier.

I have always wanted to bond with a dragon of the great lineage."

"You're not taking my bonded mythicals," I shot back. "But you're welcome to come through me to get them."

"Not a problem," he replied as his mind hit mine, so powerful as he drew on his crystals that I reeled, fell, and lost control of the air barrier.

I tumbled so fast that I was soon beneath the surface of the sandstorm. Pain flared across my skin as the tiny particles tore it and disoriented me. I continued to tumble until I found some clear air no one was connected to.

Using my main element to steady myself, I slowed and reconstructed my barrier. I was still in the middle of the sandstorm, and I had been flung off-course, but I was determined to find the dark elf and lead him farther away.

Although the storm was the perfect place to hide, I couldn't let Kirdash go toward the others. That gave me one option: I had to fly back up and challenge the dark elf. I had to keep him moving and get him to waste his energy, preferably without using much of mine.

I rose, knowing that, if nothing else, I had to get out of the battering sand. I soon found myself in the middle of the group of dark elves, Kirdash above them.

He laughed and snatched control again. This time I was ready, however, darting to the side and using my circlet to boost my powers. With his focus on me, I flew away from my mythicals, increasing the distance as I snatched the air from the dark elves.

They plummeted into the sand as I had, and I powered north and away from them. Several times I glanced back to see if Kirdash was following since his mind was still pushing mine.

He was coming after me but slowly, his amusement clear from the grin on his face and the way he held his head. This was a game to him, and I was the toy.

Frustration and fear rose inside of me. I could feel my power waning. I'd pushed hard, and Zephyr and my other mythicals were getting farther away. They were also fighting.

We're surrounded, Zephyr said a moment later. *I think we can break through, but you need to find a way to us, not get farther away. We can fight them better together.*

No. I can't bring Kirdash to you.

You can't face him alone.

I gritted my teeth. Zephyr was right. I didn't have the strength, but while I distracted Kirdash, the others could flee. There had to be a way I could win this fight.

The artifact, Zephyr replied, no longer arguing with me. *The artifact makes an elf stronger, right? Beat him to the artifact, and then come back here with it. If we all connect to it...*

It might be enough to beat him.

Exactly.

It was the closest thing we had to a plan.

Keep everyone safe and get them south, I thought.

I could feel the resistance in Zephyr's emotions, but he didn't argue. Instead, he pushed his powers out. Although I wanted to merge and help him as well, I didn't connect. I didn't want to accidentally draw energy from him to help me.

Sen, Nuri, and Roth sent waves of affection my way as they fought alongside the dragon. Sen sent me snippets now and then to show me the dark elf patrol attacking from nearby buildings.

As Kirdash came after me, he shifted from pulling the air out from under me to trying to seize control of my mind.

Although I didn't know how he could connect mentally the way he did, I fought, pushing him away from my mind by getting around his connection. It was a huge distraction from my goal, however.

I needed to find the artifact while keeping him out of my head and staying in the air. The part of the plan that was going well was the part where Kirdash was following me as I flew away from my mythicals and friends. I was protecting them from the dark elf.

Before I got much farther, however, more dark elves rose ahead of me to block my path. They were also wearing gemstones, and although I was wearing the armor I'd taken, this battle wasn't going to be simple.

The group merged their minds and worked together. They were in my way.

Growling, I darted to the side, but they blasted air my way. The armor absorbed part of the attack, which let me keep flying, but Kirdash chose that moment to attach to my mind again. Distracted, I couldn't stop him.

Quite the flier, my dear. You bonded with a dragon for a good reason. His words dripped honey but sent a chill up my spine. Although I didn't respond as I looked for a way to push him out of my head, his grip got stronger.

Now that there wasn't a portal between us, I appreciated how much it had dampened his abilities. His mind was stronger than I'd thought possible, and I could do nothing to evict him.

Why don't you slow and we'll chat? Oh, you're keeping me from your mythicals. How sweet of you. You do care about them, don't you? All four of them.

Again I didn't respond. I didn't want to help him figure out what I was doing. I had to dart to one side as the elves hurled elemental energy at me and pulled the air out from under me. A couple of times, I let them take control of a pocket of air as I grabbed another and replaced it.

That was easier than fighting, but it wasn't a good way to survive. Kirdash was controlling a lot of the elements around me, and I was nearing the edge of the sand. I could now feel his control of the storm.

It worried me. If Kirdash had planned this, we would be outplayed no matter what we did.

Do you like my handiwork? he asked, reminding me that he was still in my head. I wanted to scream at him, my mind reeling as his control crept along my bonds.

Remember what you usually do, Nuri said, the firebird's words calm and reassuring. I longed to have him on my shoulders, but he was needed where he was.

Nuri. I haven't had a chat with you in so long. I hope you're ready to return to me, Kirdash said, his voice gloating, all mock pleasure and lightheartedness. It was somehow even more chilling.

Not wanting the dark elf anywhere near my mythicals, I attacked the link between us from the side. It made him growl, but he hit my control of the air again, and I tumbled once more.

This time his dark elves followed me. The sandstorm

was less intense on this edge but still enough to make my skin burn and disorient me.

I wasn't sure what to do now. The rest of the group was far enough away to be safe.

I've managed to get Vestan and the others out. The sandstorm is dying out on this side.

That's because Kirdash is focusing it on me.

Stay away from him if you can. We're coming to you now.

No. Get yourselves safe too, I replied as another blast of air knocked me off-course.

I was reeling, still trying to find something I could grasp, mentally or otherwise, to steady myself, but Kirdash controlled everything around me, and I couldn't get through his grip.

We're coming to you, Zephyr insisted, the sick feeling in my stomach easing as my mythicals flew toward me.

Although I wanted to argue, I couldn't. I tried to figure out how high I was. The ground and buildings were coming up at an alarming rate, and I had to slow down. Pulling energy from the crystal in my circlet, I fought to grab more air, finally pushing through Kirdash's defenses.

I slowed mere feet from smacking into the roof of a building. I hovered and formed another barrier to protect my stinging skin, my head aching and my body trembling.

I couldn't see Kirdash or couldn't figure out where he was. I also knew I couldn't face him and his minions alone. I didn't have enough power left, not without help. The circlet's crystal was almost drained, and I needed to find the artifact.

Relief flooded through me as I located a powerful crystal unlike any I'd ever connected with. It wasn't far, located to the east. I flew in that direction, staying low over the buildings, letting the power the artifact contained guide me closer. Zephyr, Sen, Roth, and Nuri sped to me like bullets.

I was only yards from the artifact when Kirdash attacked my mind and control again. I managed to keep him out of my head, but I fell and hit the building below me hard. The flares of pain in my chest and legs and the cracking sounds let me know I'd broken several body parts.

The roof gave way at the impact, and I hit the floor. More pain flared in my side, and the dust and sand kicked up by my landing made me want to cough.

I couldn't move or speak, unable to process anything but the agonizing pain. My body hurt in so many places tears stung my eyes, and I had to focus on breathing.

I heard a laugh, and my mythicals sent waves of fear toward me.

Kirdash hovered above me. Something warm was flowing down my torso. Moving the arm that hurt least, I touched blood.

"You might want to do something about that. Assuming you can?" Kirdash spoke aloud for the first time.

I couldn't respond, fear gripping me as my mind went fuzzy. I was almost out of power, the circlet not having much left. I reached into my body and stopped the bleeding, assessing the damage with my mind.

There were so many broken bones and so much internal bleeding that I didn't know where to begin. I was as badly wounded as Cherisse had been, but there was no one here to help.

Kirdash chuckled as he landed, which brought my attention back to him.

"I guess you weren't the Henera after all. I'll be having one last thing from you before you die." He reached for my mind, hitting it with everything he had.

In agony and focused on stopping my bleeding, I could not keep him out. I tried pulling more from the circlet to move me away and lift off—anything to get away from him.

My mythicals were closer, but they couldn't stop Kirdash either. He felt for the bonds as he'd done so many times.

I fought, but my head blurred, aching even more, and I had nothing left. One by one, he snapped my bonds, the presence of each leaving my head like a light switching off. I whimpered in pain, unable to stop as he grinned at me.

Half-thoughts formed in my head, anger making me want to lash out, but my body was so broken I couldn't do anything.

"Zephyr," I whispered a fraction of a second before that bond broke too. Suddenly I was alone. All four of them are gone.

Zephyr, the dragon who had been there from the beginning. His presence in my life had been a constant for years.

Gone.

CHAPTER TWENTY-ONE

Kirdash flew away as I heard a roar in the distance—Zephyr. The cry turned pained and was followed by dark elves chanting "Kirdash" and "Henera."

My vision swam and my hearing faded as the sandstorm died. I continued to hold my body together with my mind, the circlet's power the only thing preventing me from dying.

Desperate to find Zephyr and the others, I reached out. I didn't care about myself or how much I hurt, I needed to find them, but I had no guide. There was no tug in my stomach to show me the direction they were in.

Although I was exhausted, I figured out what to do.

Every time I thought about my mythicals being in the hands of Kirdash, anger rose inside me, but I was weak. The circlet was running out of power, barely holding me together. I had so little left I wasn't sure if I could keep myself from bleeding out.

I needed a boost. Food, anything.

My pack had been on my back, but it wasn't now, lost

during one of my tumbles through the sky or in my crash landing. That meant I had to find something else.

I closed my eyes, my hand still pressed over my side, using pressure as well as my mental abilities to keep myself from dying. Everything still hurt, but the pain had dulled, either because I was getting used to it or I didn't have the energy to feel it. Either way, it gave me space to focus.

The pack I'd carried was not in the rubble or anywhere nearby, but I didn't have to reach very far to feel the artifact we'd come here for. I tried to connect to it, but it was out of range.

Instead, I lifted it with air, the strange orb feeling light but yet substantial. As tired as I was, it took all my strength to control the air bringing it out of the building it was in and over to me. I almost dropped it twice, and the bleeding in my side worsened as I focused everything on flying the artifact.

Before it came into view, I could see the glow it cast. It was strange to see a light come closer, and I found myself grinning at the irony of bringing light to myself when I was dying and trying not to. I began repairing my injuries.

There wasn't anyone to save me, and everyone was going to think I was dead. I had to stay alive long enough for my elven healing abilities to kick in and my power to come back.

Trying not to focus on how difficult that might be when I was so drained, I brought the orb closer. When it was still a couple of feet from me, the circlet ran out of air power, and I dropped it.

I hoped it didn't shatter when it hit the ground. Thankfully it didn't; it even bounced closer, but it came to rest against a large chunk of roof that had fallen into the room with me.

I reached for it, but it wasn't close enough, and as soon as I took my good hand from my wound, it bled more.

I had to get to the object. I could feel its power—power I could use. Power that would save my life if I lived long enough to get it working, but I was drained, and the air crystal in the circlet was too.

I tried to move, but the pain was too great. I could not drag my broken body across the ground. It wasn't going to happen, no matter how much I wanted to reach the artifact.

As I pressed my hand to my side again and connected to the circlet, desperate to find a tiny bit of air elemental magic, I realized I still had three crystals. Even if I couldn't move it with air, there might be another way to bring it over.

Reaching into the earth crystal, I drew the power I needed to reshape the ground between me and the orb, making a funnel that sloped toward my arm and hand. It took longer than I'd have liked since I also drew on the water crystal to keep myself from bleeding.

Slowly, I brought the orb toward me until it reached my hand and stopped against the back of it. It was an unconventional form of contact, but it was enough.

I reached for it with my mind, connecting to it and drawing on its power. I was flooded with what felt like energy but wasn't.

My mind awoke to the elements in a new way despite my pain and exhaustion. It didn't provide energy so much as amplify it, as Sierrathen had suggested. I couldn't draw on it, but I could use my elemental energy again.

I was worried that there wasn't enough left in the circlet to heal me, but I got to work anyway.

I didn't have a medical elf to guide me this time, but I knew the basics. The thing to stop was the bleeding. Anything infectious came second. Bones could wait. I wasn't even going to attempt to move until I was fixed.

It felt strange to be working on myself, given how light-headed and out of it I was. It gave me something to focus on, the ache in my chest and stomach partially caused by the absence of my mythicals.

Several times, I almost gave up and let myself die. I could go to sleep. Let go. Someone else could worry about fighting Kirdash. Someone else could save the day and find a way to beat him.

Like the greats who had done their best, I knew I had done everything in my power. Maybe Simon could take everything he'd learned from me and make someone who'd perform even better. Someone Minsheng could train. Someone who knew she was the Henera from the beginning.

Then I thought about Zephyr, Sen, Roth, and Nuri and how they felt right now. They weren't dying. They couldn't say goodbye. Kirdash had taken them captive, and they would be trying to get back to me. Zephyr wouldn't give up.

It gave me the strength I needed to keep going. To keep fighting the sleep that wanted to drag me under and make my body heal. Only a little longer.

Parts of me were still leaking my precious blood as I

drained the circlet of another element, then another. I had fire left; that was it.

The orb couldn't give me energy. It just made what I had more effective. I wanted to scream, but I was far too tired, and the desire to sleep for a while was overwhelming. Instead, I tried to think of a way to get more energy. My mythicals needed me. I couldn't die here, not like this.

No matter what I thought up, without elemental magic, it wouldn't work.

Time was meaningless, my mind blanking as I lay there. Now and then, I started when a breeze blew across me and tickled my cheek or a hand. Anywhere there was bare skin.

Whenever I opened my eyes again, I checked my body and used more magic to heal. Time must have passed since I could do more to repair myself, but my body still hurt, and there was so much to do.

When I stirred once more, I was even weaker, unable to see or hear. I thought of all the hopes I'd had. The times people had chanted "Henera" and bowed to me because they thought I could save them. All the people whose hopes would die with me.

Was this how the greats had felt? Had Tuviel died like this?

I wanted to look at her necklace one last time, but I couldn't lift an arm to reach it. The great artifact I could reach easily was the ring. I could stretch my good hand over to the bad one and rub my finger across it.

As I did that, I realized the great artifacts contained elemental crystals. I'd used a device to suck the energy out of them to power the pillars on a previous occasion.

Could I do that now? Could I use the artifacts of the four greats to save my life?

Not having Simon's device to make the task easier made me hesitate, but I didn't have long.

I started with the ring I was touching and focused on connecting my mind to its power. I expected to have problems, but apparently, I was getting better at connecting to artifacts. It willingly gave me its power.

I connected to the other artifacts as well. They weren't all as easy, however.

When I got back to healing, I found my concentration slipping again, the progress slow. I kept going, my mind working through the parts of me that were bleeding until I had managed to stop that.

I still didn't move despite the dryness in my mouth and my hunger. While the pain had eased and I was in less danger, I was still sporting more broken bones than I was ready to heal. Starting with the ones that would make it hard to walk, I healed my legs and then my chest.

As I fixed my ribs and collarbone, I realized how much pain they had been causing me and how difficult it had been to breathe. At some point, I must have drifted off since the sky was dark when I roused to work again.

As I fixed the last of the bones needed to move, so much time had passed that the sun was rising. My head was pounding, and I was getting dehydrated.

I used my stronger arm and my legs to get up and into a better position. While I wanted to keep healing myself, I could do that while moving. This place wasn't safe, and I had to take care of myself in other ways. Not wanting to abandon the new artifact, I tucked it into my top, nestling it against my body, then got to my feet.

It took several minutes to go from sitting to standing, and I felt dizzy and swayed. I had to hold onto the crumbling wall with one hand as I shuffled toward the door.

I needed water, and I didn't want to expend much energy to find it. Given this city was once large, there must be a water source. I had to find it.

Reaching out, I marveled at how much bigger my range was while I was connected to the orb. It made everything much easier, and I regretted not finding it sooner. It would have given me an advantage against Kirdash, and it might have prevented everything that had happened.

I paused. Normally Zephyr would have reassured me at this point. He'd have said something comforting, like how much more it mattered that I was alive and had the orb now. How I could still keep on and sort this out. Maybe he'd throw in a funny comment about pizza.

Instead, there was silence.

The city was deathly quiet. So quiet, I could hear my heart pounding to push the little blood I had left around my body. I could also hear every movement I made, but I didn't expend the energy to be quiet.

Reaching across the city, I found an underground river. Well, it was a stream now, but it was water, and it gave me something to focus on.

I walked without seeing or thinking. This old city held no fascination or interest for me. Like everything else in my life lately, it was yet another place I was passing through on my way to save someone or find something.

My insides felt empty, but I continued to repair myself

as I walked, figuring out the priority of the body parts I had left to heal. I had taken damage in many places, having hit the side of the building and the roof and then going through it and crash-landing on the floor.

The pain wasn't the worst of it, however. Losing my mythicals and having them gone from my mind was. I kept expecting to hear their thoughts or to turn a corner and see one of them, but the relief of their presence never came. I was alone, and I couldn't bear it.

Still, I trudged on. Every time I faltered and wanted to give up, I thought about how Zephyr and the others must feel and kept putting one foot in front of the other while I healed myself.

I was going to get my elementals back and make Kirdash regret starting a fight with me.

CHAPTER TWENTY-TWO

I was drinking water and resting when I realized I wasn't alone. I could feel people moving at the edges of the area my mind could detect.

They were moving cautiously as a group, and sometimes it felt as if they were hardly there. They apparently paused and went silent, seeming to melt into their surroundings before they made themselves known again.

Although I was stronger for having finished healing myself and having drunk, I didn't want to tangle with anyone yet. I started looking for a way to get past without them noticing.

It wasn't until Vestan's familiar mind reached out to check the group's surroundings that I realized they were allies, not enemies. They were sometimes difficult to detect because they were using their cloaks. Relief washed through me, but also sadness that Vestan's bird was no longer there and another soldier was missing.

I let Vestan detect my mind as I got to my feet and

made my way to the surface again. The group reacted to my presence, excitement making them move faster.

Narrowing my control, I guided them closer until I could see them weaving toward me on one of the city's main streets.

Still exhausted, I sat near the water and waited for them to join me. Vestan and Cherisse looked me over, the two being the first to reach me.

"You look like shit, Henera. What did you do, have an argument with a rock?" Cherisse asked.

As soon as she uttered my title, tears stung my eyes and fell. They didn't stop. I wasn't the Henera anymore. My four bonded mythicals were gone. All the grief, anguish, and pain at being parted from the four souls I loved most came out in sobs that tore through my torso and left me unable to stand.

Someone put their arms around me as everyone else came closer.

"We'll get them back," Cherisse said after I quieted, too exhausted to cry anymore. "You've been stubborn about helping us. We'll get them back and make him pay. I swear that every elf on Earth and every elf we find here will come with you to do so."

I didn't respond, too drained to speak. I had no idea how we were going to manage what she was promising, but I had to try. I wasn't the only one without a mythical, either. Kirdash had stolen them all.

"We need to find them," I stated when I had regained enough strength to talk.

"We will. Vestan says there's an elf at the Sanctuary who knows where Kirdash keeps the mythicals he cares about controlling. They're going to help us find all our mythicals."

I did not want to go back through a portal to the human world without my mythicals. I didn't want to answer the questions I would be asked or have to persuade others to let me run missions, but we needed food and supplies.

I was about to point out my lost pack when the major came over carrying two. He saw my gaze move to it and slipped the smaller one off his back. Blinking in shock, I took my pack from him.

"We found it on the way here. Some of the stuff inside is broken, and it took a chunk out of the side of an old fountain, but the bag survived the fall pretty well."

"I think the dark elf knocked it off me during the fight," I explained, my emotions threatening to overwhelm me again as I thought about him.

Everyone drank from the underground water source as Cherisse told me what had happened to them. Zephyr, Sen, Roth, and Nuri had helped defend everyone from a squad of powerful dark elves and managed to help them sneak out of the building they had been trapped inside.

My mythicals had then headed toward me.

Before Vestan and the others had gotten very far, however, Kirdash had rolled through. He'd taken their mythicals using mine, along with the dark elves who had attacked me.

Vestan and Cherisse had done everything they could think of and gotten the group away, but not before a tumbling building had landed on one of the soldiers. I wanted to cry with frustration, and the pain in Cherisse and the others was evident. They too had lost the mythicals they were bonded to.

And the soldiers had lost a friend. There wasn't one of us who hadn't sacrificed someone in the last twenty-four hours.

"We need to get you back to Earth," Vestan said a moment later, and Ronan slipped a hand around my waist.

"I would be honored if you would let me carry you for a while," the tall centaur said, his head lowering as he spoke.

My eyes went wide, knowing few people were ever invited to ride and that only need dictated such an act. I wanted to argue, but I swayed as I got to my feet.

He swept me up and onto his back, Vestan using his air ability to make me lighter and help Ronan get me in place.

Tears stung my eyes. Although it still felt wrong not to have my mythicals in my head, I felt less alone. I had amazing friends, and they were willing to do what was needed.

"The portal to the south is heavily guarded," Cherisse said. "We're going to have to find a way around them. I don't think we can find the Mexican one."

"Not without a dragon to fly a long distance," I replied, exhausted at the thought of having to go that far.

"Sneaking it is, then."

"My cloak is trashed," I pointed out.

"If need be, we can hide you under mine," Ronan replied. "Or Roth's. His came off as he tried to flee the bonding with Kirdash."

I gritted my teeth at the thought of the monster being in their heads, forcing his control over them without their consent.

"What can he do to them?" I asked.

"I'm not sure you want us to tell you," Ronan replied, his voice gentle. "With any luck, you'll find out when you re-bond with them. They can open up about it in their own time."

As I opened my mouth to argue, I considered his response. He was right. As much as I wanted to know, it wouldn't do me any good to dwell on something that might make it harder to rescue them. I wanted to be put through the same hell. I wanted to understand exactly how they felt.

I kept my mouth shut, nodded, and let myself be carried through the city.

Thanks to the orb and my returning magic, I could reach out around us and detect if anyone came close. Several dark elf patrols never noticed that my mind and power had brushed theirs.

One thing was very clear; the patrols were looking for us, or rather, everyone except me. They thought I was dead.

I focused on the task until we were at the edge of the city, facing the trek through the desert. We shared the last of our food, and I thanked Ronan for letting me ride.

With each passing hour, I grew stronger despite the lack of food. I would survive this as long as we got to the gate.

Around noon, we opted to sleep until nightfall, wanting the dark to help hide us. Everyone agreed to take a watch in pairs, one of the five elves and one of the remaining soldiers having to watch for three-quarters of an hour while everyone else slept.

Everyone insisted I take the last watch, and I didn't have the strength to argue. Despite all the thoughts in my head and how worried I was, my body was exhausted, and I fell asleep immediately. I awoke to a feeling of guilt.

The stars shone overhead, and everyone else was sitting nearby, wide awake. I sat up quickly, and Cherisse came over and gave me a hand up.

"Don't apologize or beat yourself up. We all opted to let you rest longer. It was selfish of us, but we're going to need your abilities, Henera."

Cherisse's words stopped me in my tracks. There was something lovely about being told not to apologize. I wasn't sure they'd let me sleep for their benefit, but it would help us all if I could use my abilities to better effect.

I reached out to see what lay ahead. The patrols had stopped, and I was grateful to know that none had come close while I'd slept. There were elves between us and the portal, however.

None of us wanted to tangle with more dark elves, but there was only one way for us to get home. That meant we had no choice but to get past them.

With that in mind, we trudged south. Thanks to the orb, a task that had once required Sen's sight was a lot easier. It let me monitor the locations of the dark elves as we moved and make sure we always knew where they were and what they were controlling.

I called a halt, and we hid under our cloaks when a patrol came too close. It worked wonderfully, getting us closer to the portal even if it took longer. We had to stop more frequently the nearer we got.

It was clear they were either guarding this portal or

preparing for another attack through it, however, as there were more than fifty dark elves near it. I wasn't sure how we were going to get past so many, especially when we had no backup. This was the whole team.

When it was clear we could go no farther without being discovered, I halted us again and we huddled, using our cloaks to become a hidden mass in the dark. I formed a barrier around us to keep any noise in so we could come up with a plan.

"There are twenty on the gate," I said. "And another four groups of eight roaming around, each one an element."

"We're going to have to distract some of them," Cherisse replied. "Only way we'll get through."

None of us could argue with her logic, so we had to come up with suitable distractions. I was drawing a blank.

Anything big needed one of us, probably me, to use my powers. Having an elemental elf use her abilities nearby would be a beacon. I wasn't sure what to do about that.

"We've got explosives," the major offered. "What if we blow something up? Get a timer. We can put it on one side so they go there to investigate and come around the other side. Then we hit whoever is left on the gate with everything we've got left."

I frowned. It might work, but the twenty elves on the gate wouldn't move, even if the four mobile squads took the bait. Could I take on twenty dark elves with four elves for backup?

If I'd had a bunch of crystals, my circlet, and my mythicals, I wouldn't have hesitated. Today, when part of my soul had been ripped out, I wasn't sure about anything.

While the soldiers and Seth talked about how they could make a big explosion and what could be done to harness the fire elements along with it, I tried to figure out what I might be able to do. My mind wouldn't function.

Everyone was staring at me, and I realized I had frozen. I was normally the one to make the final decision and give the commands, but I couldn't right now.

Cherisse stepped in. "Let's do this. We can handle whatever follows. We have to for the sake of our mythicals."

The last sentence was supposed to prod me to get my shit together. I wanted to ignore it since it was designed to get me angry and fire me up, but it did as intended. Zephyr, Sen, Roth, and Nuri needed me.

"Okay," I said, then took a deep breath. "I'm going to bury any dark elves who get between us and that portal."

"That's our Henera!" Cherisse exclaimed as she broke from the huddle.

It was more violent and aggressive than what I was used to, but I was done playing nice. These dark elves were enslaving mythicals and destroying a planet. There came a point where peaceful methods were no longer an option. We could do nothing except remove the problem in the most efficient manner.

I'd gotten to that point. Anyone standing between me and my mythicals was going to find out how lethal I could be.

CHAPTER TWENTY-THREE

It had taken several hours, but we were finally in position and ready for the explosion. We'd wanted to give ourselves plenty of time, so we still had another half an hour to wait. I didn't mind having longer to recharge my abilities.

As we sat, I felt around the portal, figuring out the patterns of the twenty dark elves who were likely to stay and inching as close to them as I dared get.

The rest of the elves hung back with the soldiers and our centaur so they weren't detected, but I was sure the orb would keep me from being felt.

Of course, there was a chance that the rest of the dark elves would stay put as well, which would make the battle pretty much impossible unless I could bury the first twenty elves so quickly we could rush through the portal and get to safety on the other side.

That was the other big unknown. The portal on the other side was supposed to be partially reopened as we arrived.

Unless that could be done quickly, we ran the risk of

getting squashed or sent back through the portal to the waiting dark elves. I also didn't want to lead the dark elves to Earth if there wasn't a solid defense there.

I couldn't control any of that, however. All I could do was wait for the signal, then kill the dark elves.

Time ticked by as I moved to an optimal position and huddled under Roth's cloak. It smelled faintly of the pegasus and the salty water, which was both comforting and heart-wrenchingly painful. I would make sure it got back to its owner soon, however.

Ready to snatch control of elements and use them, I waited. My stomach was in a knot from anxiety and hunger. I hadn't eaten very much since we'd been gone, and we'd been gone for a lot longer than we'd hoped. It wasn't ideal.

The timer finished its countdown, and a fireball rose on the horizon, drawing everyone's attention. The sky lit up a moment before the noise was audible, the boom so loud it made my ears ring. Several of the dark elves lifted their hands to shield their ears.

The next thing to hit was the shockwave. The air rushed toward us in a heated wave, bringing debris with it. I used an air barrier to shield myself from the worst of it, grateful Vestan would do the same for everyone else. Then I waited some more.

This was crunch time. What else would happen, and how would the dark elves respond? A moment later, there was a set of smaller bangs. Gunshots, the triggers rigged to be set off by secondary timers I didn't understand, involving gunpowder and Seth's abilities.

The second element had the desired impact. The dark

elf units ran toward the roaring flames and gunshots, taking the bait.

I waited long enough for the dark elf patrols to be out of sight, then moved on to the other twenty elves. With the five earth elementals, I lifted them into the air and put boxes around each of their heads, stealing their oxygen.

With the other fifteen, I dropped the ground out from beneath them until they were ten feet down, then piled it back in on top of them. I held it there with the elements.

The rest of my team ran up, not noticing me until I threw back my cloak's hood. I had singlehandedly killed twenty dark elves.

"You did find a powerful artifact," Vestan said as he took in the five bodies I'd laid on the ground and the disturbed earth that was the grave of the other fifteen.

"Let us hope it can fuel my fury long enough to get all our mythicals back," I replied. I wasn't sure Zephyr would approve of what I was doing to get to him, but I didn't care.

While the dark elves all breathed their last, I got to my feet. It was time to go home before any more dark elves appeared. Then I was going to do everything I could to get my mythicals back.

I strode to the sand dune ahead of us, able to see the portal shimmering but also feeling with my mind.

"I want you all to go through first. Earth elf, then soldiers, then Ronan, then the rest of the elves."

No one argued, but I sounded angry enough that no one would have dared, even if they had other ideas. They hurried to the portal and slipped through.

I walked after them, making sure the area was safe, then I followed them to the other side.

Grateful that we'd managed this part of our adventure well, I stepped into the glowing circle of light. I had been suspended in the portal for long enough to get emotional and upset again, the thought of leaving Zephyr, Sen, Roth, and Nuri behind on another planet breaking my heart once more.

If I'd been able to cry while I was in the portal, I would have sobbed, but as it was, I just ached and had an over-whelming desire to let it out.

When I emerged from the portal, there was a dim light in the open space ahead of me. I wanted to seem strong in front of elves I didn't know well, but as soon as Minsheng came toward me, my resolve broke. The wide-eyed yet pained look on his face told me everything. He'd been told.

He wrapped his arms around me as I broke. Cherisse and Vestan came down the tunnel.

"We should get out of here and bury the portal again," Vestan said, his words calm and gentle. Cherisse slipped an arm around me and guided me away.

Although I didn't want to move, I allowed myself to be guided. I had to keep everyone safe.

As we walked away, I used my mind and abilities to close the area, bringing dirt in around the portal and making the blockage larger and denser as I backed toward the surface.

It didn't take long. Other earth elves merged their abili-ties with mine to get it done. I wasn't sure if it was good or bad to be done so swiftly, but the site was now safe from Kirdash.

Others shot me sorrowful looks as I left the tunnel. I didn't meet anyone's gaze, not wanting their pity or anything else. Soon, it wouldn't matter. I would get them back. No one was going to get in my way.

I stopped at the tents outside the portal building long enough to get food. I let everyone from the Sanctuary know I intended to go there next, then repacked my go-bag while stuffing my face. I didn't plan on sleeping but heading straight for whichever refugee could tell me where I was most likely to find my mythicals.

I was cramming in bread when Minsheng strode in.

"I've got the major, the powerful elves, Ronan, and as many soldiers as we think we can get away with ready and waiting in the vehicles," he said with no other explanation for what was going on.

"What for?" I asked.

"They're going with you, of course. We're all going to help get those mythicals back. Ours or not, they're family."

I gulped, having not considered how someone like Minsheng might feel in this situation. I almost refused their help. I didn't want them putting themselves in danger when I hadn't managed to protect the last group of mythicals who had gone into battle with me.

It was an interesting challenge to navigate. I wanted to go alone, but I had a higher chance of success if I didn't. The truth was, I needed the help, and I didn't have the strength to argue.

But I wasn't sure I wanted to go in a vehicle when I could fly there quicker. However, the point of being a team was to stick together, and that meant finding something that worked for all of us and got us there at a reasonable speed.

I nodded and let Minsheng put extra snacks and

anything else he thought would be useful in my pack. It would have been adorable had I not been in a hurry and focused on leaving.

He picked up on my desire to hurry, however, and quickly got the job done, putting in more snack bars in my bag than I usually carried but leaving everything else much the same.

As I finished repacking it, I was grateful to the major for finding it for me. It would have been an extra blow to lose the pack as well.

Soon I was bundled in the back of an Army truck, allies and friends on either side of me as we set off for the Sanctuary.

A direct flight wouldn't have been easy, but it was also not an option this time. That said, I appreciated the chance to rest. The task at hand was pressing, but I would need the energy. If I'd flown to the Sanctuary with my elemental power, I'd have drained myself.

No one spoke to me, and I felt their avoidance when I looked at someone. Some felt pity, but most didn't appear to know what to say. I couldn't blame them. I didn't know what to say or think either, other than to do everything I could to go get my mythicals back.

I snacked as I rode and tried not to think about anything except plans and who I might ask to come with me and what they could do. Cherisse, Seth, Vestan, and Serfina were with me again. All of them had lost mythicals too. Their hurt was my hurt.

Minsheng and Daisy had made it clear they were coming with me as well, and Ronan wanted to. The major couldn't leave without the general's approval, and he'd lost men on the last mission. Although the general frequently supported me, he didn't have the same stakes in the battle, and he'd lost more people.

The elves had ways of surviving, healing, and moving faster. The soldiers were more likely to die. I didn't know how to help with that, other than to get more of the armor we'd been appropriating into their hands.

While we drove to the Sanctuary, I napped, much to my relief and the relief of everyone with me. Ronan had used his mental link with the other centaurs at the Sanctuary to tell them what had happened and ask them our questions.

When I stepped out of the back of the truck, we had a welcome party. Almost every strong elf in the Sanctuary, every centaur, and every dwarf who guarded the border was there. Several vehicles were ready to go, although some looked as if they'd seen better days.

"We've spoken to the refugees," Gwaelon said as he came up to me. "They're not fit to come with us, and I wouldn't ask them to go back to that planet and face something this traumatic, but they described what they knew of the most likely compound in detail. With help from the centaurs and the dwarves, we've got a mental picture to work with. If you allow it, Henera, I'd like to be your guide. We'd all like to rescue the mythicals who have fought for us so many times."

I didn't know what to say as I looked at all the eager faces. This wasn't going to be an easy journey, and it would be dangerous. There were elves here who had mythicals to lose, Newton sitting on Erlan's shoulder and other creatures beside or on other elves. This wasn't without risk to those mythicals as well.

I just nodded. This wasn't what I'd expected.

The moment I gave the affirmative, the mythicals sprang into action, heading toward their vehicles.

"We think the closest portal is the one you found open in Ireland," Gwaelon continued. "The one in Greenland might work, but we have a feeling that one will draw more attention and take us longer."

Orthelo stepped up. "And we think you can return through a nearer portal, but we need to get it open first."

"Well, and find it," Aquilan added.

I lifted an eyebrow, not sure we wanted any more portals open.

"The second we take these mythicals, the dark elf is going to attack with everything he has," Minsheng interjected when he saw me open my mouth. "There's no point in making it so he can't get to us. We're going to have to fight him, and there's nothing any of us can do except tip the odds in our favor. Getting our mythicals back will do that."

My heart swelled in my chest at the support I had, but fear made me shake.

"We'll get them all back, and then we'll make sure Kirdash pays," I said a moment later. "But we're going to need every bit of help we can get. Every artifact, every crystal, every tablet, every bit of technology, armor, and every weapon and snack this army can lay its hands on."

"You'll have it," Cherisse said as she joined me, the major beside her. "Simon is working with dwarves and gnomes on a bunch of stuff. The general called to let us know there is a large plane waiting to pick us up at the nearest airport, and the organization has a supply convoy heading to the farm in Ireland to meet us."

"And we've brought every artifact we've found," Aquilan said, holding up what looked like a fan. "Throwing blade. It's an air artifact. Nothing flies as true as this does. It's...lethal."

I lifted my eyebrows as he handed it over. I could feel the connection it wanted. It pulled at my mind, but it didn't seem to want power. It was full.

That was the last of the revelations, and it helped me focus on the task at hand. All I had to do was persuade another dragon to let my horde descend from his mountain and go get a bunch of mythicals back.

CHAPTER TWENTY-FOUR

The flight felt as if it took forever, despite managing to sleep more. I thought about the mission we were about to go on. Minsheng was right; no matter how well this went, it was likely to trigger a huge battle with Kirdash. I had to be ready for that.

I didn't feel ready, but I had put my spare energy into the crystals in my circlet, and I could see elves around me filling other crystals and tablets as we flew, many of them well-rested and able to regenerate by the time we needed to fight.

There were more suits of armor among us than I'd expected. We had a lot more soldiers as well. Almost the entire force from the Texas portal site was on the plane with us, two hundred mythicals and humans in total. There was a gun for everyone, plus an Army pack with basic gear like a flashlight, a canteen, and a pocket knife.

When we landed, darkness had descended, but when I approached the farm, it was buzzing with activity. Iris was waiting for me at the gate, with the farmer beside her.

The farmer's gaze roved over the army with me, then he glanced at Iris, but he wasn't angry or upset. Then I noticed the truck in the farmyard outside the barn. The back was open, and several people were pulling out boxes of rations, snacks, and water bottles and placing them in clear plastic bags.

"You seem to be expecting us," I said, boggling at what must have happened before I'd arrived.

"You could say that. The dragon isn't, though. Not yet. We sent one o' the lads through to him, but he's in the sky and not back yet."

"Let me go see if I can find him," I replied. "Please get everyone else what they need while I do. He might take it better if I tell him how many people want to come to his domain."

I left everyone behind and headed to the barn, still in shock about what was happening and who I had to work with. None of this was going to succeed without the cooperation of a dragon who didn't like our kind.

With that in mind, I wasn't going to feel like this could happen until I'd spoken to him.

I found the portal shimmering in the dark and a couple of farm lads standing in front of it holding lanterns.

"He's on the way," the young man nearest the portal said.

"What did you tell him?"

"That you were here and urgently needed to talk to him. That's what the woman outside said would be best."

"Thank you. You can get some rest now," I replied as I moved to the side to let them out of the barn door.

They hurried away, not thinking to leave the lantern. I stood in the dark, but then I lifted my hand and started a fire in the palm, making sure it didn't burn me. It didn't light the barn much, but it was enough to see, and it wasn't too taxing.

I considered going through the portal to the dragon, but there was a good chance he was on his way here, so I had to wait. I could make things worse by being clever, so I remained on this side.

It proved to be the right call since he came through a minute or two later in human form, as he had been every time I'd seen him.

"I don't like being summoned, elf," he said, his tone deep and foreboding.

"I apologize if it came across as a summons. I didn't ask for anyone to go through to you before I arrived. I was happy to go through the portal and wait for you to return from your travels instead of bringing you here."

"Well, I'm here now. You better have a good reason for being here at this late hour." The dragon looked around as if he'd just noticed we were alone. "Where are your mythicals? The other dragon."

"That's why I'm here," I replied. "He's taken them."

His gaze snapped back to my face.

"He broke the bonds and stole them. I need to go get them back."

"He bested you in combat?"

I paused before nodding. It hurt to admit it, but it was true.

"How? The power you possess emanates from you in waves."

I didn't respond at first. I'd expected shame and derision, not shock and questions about how it was possible.

"He conjured a sandstorm and I went to scout above it, not realizing it was unnatural. Not wanting to leave our comrades unprotected, Zephyr stayed behind. When I rose above it, Kirdash struck. He blasted me farther from my allies, and I'd drained much of my magic to protect everyone else."

"You gave to others and didn't keep enough for yourself?"

"I didn't expect the dark elf to attack me. Even if I had been at full capacity as I am now, he wore many crystals and artifacts. He had an almost endless well to draw from."

The dragon nodded as if he understood exactly what I was describing.

"So, you have come to Nerik. For more crystals?"

"No. Although I wouldn't say no to any you'd be willing to donate, I would not dare ask right now. Instead, I wish to cross your domain to go retrieve my mythicals. I cannot bear the thought of them being enslaved to his whims, and I cannot get there any other way as swiftly."

"You know I will grant your request. Why do you have to ask?"

"There are others who have come to aid me in this task. Some lost mythicals and hope to retrieve them."

The dragon frowned and studied me. "How many?"

"Almost two hundred."

"You dare to bring an entire army through my lands? You would command so many on such a dangerous mission?"

"I don't command any of them," I replied, feeling even

less than worthy of this task. How was I going to convince this dragon that I was a leader worthy of honor and respect when I couldn't even manage a mission independently?

"Two hundred volunteered?"

"Yes. Even human soldiers who answer to a general here on Earth and weren't commanded to help but chose to."

Before my eyes, the dragon bowed low.

"My biggest issue with the great elves of old was that they arrogantly commanded everyone around them. They believed every other mythical on the planet was here to do their bidding. Although they rode into battle, they rode in the middle of an army that gave their lives and protected them. You are not like those elves."

"I would never assume I could command anyone, least of all mythicals who have fought a tyrant to keep their freedom."

"And you are willing to face the dark elf alone. Or a cantankerous old dragon."

I smiled when he did, his last words showing understanding and warmth.

"If your army follows you into battle to rescue these mythicals willingly, and you will fight at their front, you are more the Henera than anyone who came before you."

"I always head into danger first. How else will I keep those I care about alive?" I replied. "And I'd face Kirdash a thousand times to save my mythicals, even if he breaks my body again and again."

The dragon's eyebrows rose.

"It sounds as if there is more to your tale than you have told. I would hear it from you, but let us get this army of yours on the road. I will ride with you and bear you into this battle if you'll allow me the honor of flying a great elf."

I was struck dumb. Many thought about the honor of fighting alongside me or being with me, but the truth was, I was the blessed and honored one every moment I wasn't alone.

"I would never ask such a thing of you, but I am beyond touched that you would offer. I gladly accept so I can preserve my magic and use it to defend those who need it."

"Good, you have sense, too. Come, let us get this army of yours moving."

Without looking back to see if I followed, the dragon strode toward the barn door and out into the night air. The mythicals with me were gathering extra rations, repacking their bags, and preparing to go through the portal. The US Army had provided several devices on wheels that could easily be carried by a squad of soldiers.

The dragon looked over everything that was being provided and the army I had. I was expecting his reaction to be less than impressed, but it was the opposite.

"Those of you who are ready," he boomed, "may come through to my lands. Your Henera and I will go with you to the mythicals you seek to rescue and ensure you succeed."

Gwaelon stepped forward and bowed low.

"I have been given a mental image by an elf who once resided near the prison we seek. I have offered to act as a guide, and I will make my offer again if I can be of service."

"If the Henera trusts you to guide her, so be it. You will ride with us."

Gwaelon's mouth dropped open, mirroring my own.

"I never hoped to meet one of the great dragons in my

lifetime, but now, not only have I met two, I have been offered something far more amazing. You have made an old elf ready to die happy."

"Given our mission, I hope your words don't come true. We will face the strongest dark elves, if not Kirdash."

"Then we will face them with strength and together," Gwaelon replied.

Everyone around us repeated the last word, then chanted "Together" and "Strength" as if they were their new mantras. People added "Henera," and the farmyard filled with voices raised in unison. The battle cry spoke of everything we stood for and what we meant to each other. Together, we were strong.

This satisfied the dragon, and he led the way back through the portal. I went to follow him, but as soon as we got to the portal, he stopped and took another look at me.

"Lead your army, Henera. Show us what you've become."

I grinned, feeling the pressure but also the support. Kirdash wasn't going to know what hit him. He might have bested me in the skies above a sandstorm with ten dark elves to aid him, but I was bringing an army.

If he was there, I was going to show him what true power looked like.

As we traveled through the portal, I thought of the scenarios we might encounter and how we were going to get everyone down the mountain to the compound. The truth was, it was going to be a trek, one that would take several days.

Our earth elves would make the journey easier on us, and the water elves would get us enough fresh water as we traveled. The rest would be able to help hide our passing and keep us warm at night. Any spare energy would be funneled into crystals and tablets so we could fight with even more skill and power.

It wasn't a complete plan, but I would have a couple of days to put the rest together—assuming Kirdash didn't see us coming and bring the fight to us. I was looking forward to that opportunity, but I wasn't sure I wanted to face him in the open while he had my mythicals at his side and was willing to use them in battle.

The hope was that we would take our mythicals back while they were in the prison, and I'd break Kirdash's bonds with them before he could get to us.

Of course, I was used to life not going to plan, so I made sure I had an idea for every eventuality. I hoped my friends would also have ideas.

When we got to the other side of the portal, the dragon not far behind me, it was almost dawn on this planet, and a couple of dwarves were waiting for us.

They had more crystals in their hands, embedded in a bracelet. As soon as they saw the dragon, they brought it over.

"You made this for me?" I asked when the dragon motioned for them to give it to me.

"I figured you'd be back for more power-storing crystals when you realized how many Kirdash has. I assumed you'd be bringing something to trade, but I think, given the situation, you better have it anyway."

"I won't forget this," I replied as I took it and bowed to him as a centaur would.

"We've got to win a war first, one that has been waged over millennia. I won't count my chickens."

I chuckled at the common expression. It must go back a long time.

"We'll see if we can make it happen together."

"Aye, together. It seems your army has decided that's how it will be. My line of dragons has stood alone for long enough. We are close to dying out. If we can bring something better to this world by our last acts, it will be a fitting end."

The sadness in his voice stayed any reply I might have made, but he didn't dwell or linger on it. Instead, he swept everyone before us and issued instructions to fetch things and to get us ready to move out.

As my army came through the portal, I led them to dwellings on the mountain, and we made our final preparations. The earth elves needed to carve a path down the mountain. It didn't take long for everyone to be ready. No one was shy about volunteering or helping in any way needed.

It was time to go get our mythicals back.

CHAPTER TWENTY-FIVE

Two days had passed as we walked and rode toward our destination. Gwaelon was riding on Ronan, the great centaur leading a small group of strong, fast mythicals who scouted ahead and made sure we were moving in the right direction.

I was on the back of the golden dragon, the sensation odd because I couldn't read his mind and know what he intended to do before he did it. It wasn't too dissimilar, however, and I got used to flying on his back as I had on Zephyr's.

One thing we had agreed on was that I wouldn't use my abilities to aid us if it was not needed. Instead, I funneled power into the crystals on my circlet and bracelet. I filled them equally, scared one might get knocked off in battle, or something else might happen.

I'd also made sure I was wearing and had put more power into the many artifacts I had been given. The newest artifacts we had found were borne by the mythicals below me, and others had been lost along with my bonded mythicals, but I was so powered up that I had an advantage over any elf.

Finally, I was wearing one of the suits of armor that I had appropriated from a female dark elf. Daisy had adjusted it for me, so it was a good fit.

If battle came to me, I would be ready for it.

We were still half a day's walk from the prison, however, going by what we could see from the sky and everything Gwaelon had seen in the memories of the rescued elves. There was a smudge on the horizon that was probably the prison, but we were still too far away to be sure.

"Want to fly ahead and check what that is?" the dragon beneath me asked, his voice booming so he could be heard above the whistling wind.

"Yes, but let's not get close if we can help it. I don't want them to have much warning."

"We're not likely to be able to avoid it unless we move at night," he said, reminding me that this mission was less than ideal. Unlike the last time I had broken mythicals and friends out of a compound, I didn't have Sen to scout ahead and show us what we were heading into. We would walk into this one blind.

We flew closer, the smudge becoming more distinct, though I was sure the dragon could see it better.

"That's one of his palaces," the dragon said.

"Palace? I thought it was a prison?"

"They're not different if you're him."

I gulped, wondering what it must be like for many on

this world. He kept them frightened and downtrodden. It was awful, and I didn't know why there hadn't been uprisings over the years. Why had the elven population not overthrown him?

He was only so powerful.

I and the most powerful elves I knew had beaten him back on many occasions. It might have been through the portal, but we had beaten him nonetheless.

Then I thought about how easily he'd beaten me with the right strategy and the right group of dark elves. I was the single most powerful elf other than him, and I had been left bleeding out and broken on the ground.

I shuddered, the pain so fresh in my mind that I could barely cope with the memories. So much trauma had happened in the last few years of my life. It would have made many others give up.

"If we get much closer, they'll see us. Not much flies around here, not unless it wants to find itself imprisoned or eaten."

The dragon beneath me shuddered as well, and I wondered if he had as many traumatic memories as I did. Or more. After all, his ancestors had lived on this planet with Kirdash the whole time.

"Head back to the others. We'll attack as soon as everyone is ready."

The dragon didn't need any persuading to fly back the way he'd come, but as he was turning, I thought I saw something in the sky above the palace. If it had been present, it wasn't when I glanced again, but I had an uneasy feeling. There was a chance we'd been spotted.

If we had, there was nothing we could do about it now. We had to get ready for the fight and hope it was enough.

When we reached the group, Nerik landed, and I got off. We'd been in the air for a while, and I never wanted to take his strength for granted. I let him rest as often as he wished.

He turned back into his human form, but before we could do much other than get some food, the centaurs came toward us. They were running hard, and I wondered if they'd seen something. When I looked behind them, I answered my own question.

There were either elves or a lot of mythicals in the air and more on the ground, and they were heading straight for us.

"Attack," I called when I was sure.

Everyone fell into battle formations. We'd talked about what to do if we were attacked and formed a plan, but it depended on what was coming.

Nerik turned back into a dragon as I reached for my pack and the artifacts I hadn't been wearing. As elves around me reached for tablets or crystals and the earth elves threw up physical walls for the soldiers to hide behind, I rose into the air.

I moved toward the head of the group, putting an air barrier across them and making it cold. It wouldn't hold up against a huge barrage, but it would keep my small army safer for longer.

That done, I flew ahead to get a better look at what was coming our way. There was an army of mythicals and elves, and if I wasn't seeing things, Kirdash was coming our way too.

I could have sworn it was him, but he wasn't flying on the back of any creature. Zephyr wasn't in the sky, even if other elves were flying and there were winged mythicals.

If Sen, Roth, and Nuri were in the group rushing toward us, I couldn't see them either, but I wouldn't wait to find out.

"Target the dark elves," I told the soldiers, spotting the armor we'd seen elsewhere on most of them. Bullets went through their armor, but it stored elemental attacks and threw them back at us.

That left Kirdash and the mythical creatures.

"Can you break the bonds the way Kirdash does?" the dragon asked as he flew beside me and flapped his wings slowly to match my pace.

I marveled at his skill before he lifted and circled overhead. I didn't know if I could do what he asked, but I had to try.

"Elves, try to stop the mythical creatures from hurting anyone. Centaurs, you're on defense and medical running. Dwarves and gnomes, crystals and tablet distribution, tech that might help, and aid me."

That left few people without orders, and they knew what they had to do: get any mythicals we freed safe and as far from Kirdash as possible.

I rose as well, knowing that left one target: the dark elf. He and I had unfinished business. I needed to work out how to break his bonds. No one could take him on but me.

Knowing I had to face Kirdash made my stomach knot and my body tense. There was no one to tell me to calm down, no warm voice inside my head cheering me on.

Zephyr was nearby, and I needed to find him and get him back.

I flew ahead of the group and made it clear I was waiting for Kirdash, then hovered. Flying above and ahead of the others left me vulnerable, but I was making a statement. I wanted the dark elf to take me on.

I reached out and made sure I held onto the area around me. If Kirdash wanted to knock me out of the air, he was going to have to try hard.

No sooner had I reached my control out than the elves behind me merged their minds with mine, making all of us stronger. I hadn't asked or expected the others to stand with me, but it made me feel braver.

I might not have my mythicals, but I wasn't alone.

Kirdash and his army came closer, many of them marching along the road toward us but some in the air. There were mythical creatures with him too, and they spread out as they got closer. Birds, fire foxes, a pegasus or two, and other creatures I recognized. Dryads of different shapes and sizes brought up the rear.

They looked unhappy, and they moved with their heads down, bodies dirty and feathers askew. These weren't mythicals like the creatures on our side of the fight. Ours held their heads high, and their bodies were taken care of.

Anger rose inside me at how many of the mythicals must be hurting and were being used against their will. This wasn't how battles were supposed to be fought. This wasn't how elves were supposed to bond.

I rose even higher.

"Kirdash, enough is enough," I called, using the air to

project my voice. "Return all the mythicals you have stolen and free the elves you've enslaved."

He laughed as he flew closer, and his army continued to advance. No one challenged our control but stopped at the edge of it.

"I won't say it again, Kirdash. You don't hold enough power to stop me. I will take back my mythicals and free the others by force if I have to."

"Bold words from someone I've beaten once."

"And left for dead. Still, here I am. This time, I'm not alone."

I pushed at his control. Although he tried to keep the arrogant look of disdain and confidence on his face, his expression wavered as I piled on the pressure.

Rather than waiting for him to reach out for my mind, I reached for his. I had nothing to lose and wanted to make sure he knew what it felt like to be challenged for once. His mind fought it, but the army was merged with me, and I reached for the circlet and bracelet I wore.

It boosted me enough that I pushed past his defenses and into his head. I gasped as the anger, hurt, and darkness in his head almost overwhelmed me.

I heard him laughing in my head a moment later.

Surprised by what you see, my dear? It's hard being in the heads of others. As he spoke, he showed me images, memories of things he'd done to people and elves. Rape, torture, and pain. He was pure evil, his pain soothed by inflicting it on his prey.

My control slipped as he probed me, but a battle cry of "Henera" from below helped me remember what I was here to do.

Pushing back, I reached beyond his memories to find what bound him to the mythicals. Before I could break the bonds, he ordered his army to attack.

They didn't hesitate despite us being strong and entrenched in our positions. My mind and the combined control I had with the other elves was battered hard, along with the barrier I'd thrown up.

It took all my strength to hold on as the soldiers opened fire to take out their targets. They were surprisingly effective; Kirdash's dark elves did not expect bullets despite our previous battles. Several of the dark elves went down, which lessened the attack on me.

I renewed my assault on the dark elf's mind, pushing toward the bonds as his mythicals joined the battle. Some of them bounced off the air barrier I'd created, unable to get through but straining our minds as we held it. The birds flew around and over, however, and dived at the soldiers.

Several elves blasted them away, not wanting to do more than defend when these creatures would be docile if they were free. As soon as I attacked the bonds again, Kirdash hit me with his mind, attacking my path to him. I strained against the powerful attack, stretched in many directions.

When I didn't break, Kirdash flew closer, closing the gap between us. I was sure he intended to make my job harder, but the closest soldiers decided that it brought him within range, and they fired at him.

Most of their bullets bounced off his shield, but one got through and hit his arm. I felt his pain across our connection, but it was muted, and he was distracted by it enough that I managed to break his bond with several of the birds.

They fell out of the sky as if they no longer knew how to fly. One of the air elves used our merged powers to catch them and set them down.

It wasn't huge progress, but it gave us an advantage. The right advantage was all we needed to win this battle.

CHAPTER TWENTY-SIX

The fight continued for several more minutes. I broke a bond here and there while everyone else waged war below Kirdash and me. Occasionally the dark elf tried to hit me or fly at me, but I dodged, keeping him roughly the same distance away.

Now and then, he grabbed a bond back, forcing whatever poor mythical creature we'd rescued to do his will. Most had been collected by Minsheng and Daisy, and the birds had been placed in cages. However, it was a dangerous job, and not all the mythicals were close to our lines when I broke the bonds.

I was beginning to tire, the battle so fierce I could feel other elves waning. On top of that, the tablets were running out of power. If we weren't careful, the tide of this battle could easily turn back in Kirdash's favor. We needed something unexpected to happen, or Kirdash might win after all.

The earth elves with us were repairing a section of the

wall protecting our soldiers when Kirdash zoomed past me and hit it with everything he had. The attack blew it up, and several soldiers went flying.

Growling, I attacked the air he controlled and pulled it out from under him to protect my friends and allies. Given that he was distracted, I thought I'd manage it, but he reacted to my attack and pulled up and away, his crystals fueling him.

I needed help to fend him off as I moved over the hurting soldiers and helped the earth elves rebuild the wall in record time. That gave Kirdash time to recover and recapture the bonds I'd broken.

I glanced below to get an idea of how well the battle was going, but it was worse than I'd hoped. Although the soldiers had taken out some of the dark elves and I had allowed us to capture and keep some of the mythicals out of Kirdash's reach, several soldiers were hurt too badly to keep fighting, and our elves were running out of power.

Even with the armor they wore, our team was harder hit. This battle needed a surprise, something I couldn't provide.

No sooner had I thought this than the great golden dragon who had carried me this far dove from the sky. With him came a flock of birds. Kirdash's eyes widened when the shadow of the enormous creature fell over him.

Nerik didn't hesitate to attack, raking his claws across Kirdash's chest and exhaling the paralyzing gas I'd seen Zephyr produce on many occasions.

I reached out to control the white vapor, moving it closer to the dark elves and knocking them out. The birds with Nerik swooped and drove off the mythicals, forcing them to one side and away from Kirdash as well as us.

I left Kirdash and my allies for a moment to concentrate on knocking out the attacking elves. It took longer to work than I'd anticipated, but eventually it did, and the elves were on the ground, unable to move.

Kirdash roared his rage as the dragon swooped on him a third time. I returned my attention to him. Before I could do anything to attack the dark elf, however, he rose and flew away from the battle.

Sure my army could finish the battle, I flew after Kirdash to find an avenue to attack him. However, he either found more power somewhere or grew desperate enough to throw everything he had left at me because he lashed out hard at my control of the air.

I reeled, feeling like I'd been hit, and some of the elves who were allied with me reeled back too. This had hurt them as well. Given how high I was, I had time to catch myself, but it put more distance between Kirdash and me.

As I climbed again, the dragon swooped in to attack the dark elf. Kirdash didn't move, and at the last minute, something happened to Nerik. He bellowed and screeched and dove to the side.

Not sure what had happened, I flew at Kirdash, challenging his control and his bonds once more. I was tired, but I had to keep pushing. Just a little more, and he'd be standing alone against me and what strength was left in my allies.

I reached into his mind, sure I wouldn't see what he'd done to Nerik any other way. To my surprise, I found that the dragon was in his mind too. I could feel him like I felt Zephyr.

You forced a bond with Nerik, I said into Kirdash's head.

The dark elf turned to me and laughed.

I attacked the bond with everything I had, breaking it the same way that Kirdash had taken Zephyr from me. Now that I'd learned how it wasn't hard, but Kirdash fought me. I'd caught him off-guard, however, and he reeled as Nerik let out another roar, this one angry.

Nerik flew in our direction, hurtling past me as I hung in the air and broke more bonds while the dark elf was in shock.

One by one, mythicals were freed until he was barely controlling any near us. I didn't stop there, dodging his attacks as he dodged mine and the dragon's.

He looked at the battle below us once more and snarled. Then there was a huge blast and an attack on my mind, every crystal on Kirdash's body glowing. My mind was pushed out of his and I was flung back, my control gone and pain searing into my head.

I tumbled as Kirdash flew away, picking up speed as he ordered his army to retreat.

Most of his army was in no position to obey, but I had to focus on grabbing the air around me and slowing down before I hit the ground. Eventually, I came to a stop yards above the earth. By the time I did, Kirdash was a long way away, and I could not catch up.

Some of his dark elves fled as well, and the soldiers and elves with me went to chase them, but I held my hand out as I landed.

"No," I said. "Let them go. They're not heading for the

compound where the mythicals are. We need to rescue our friends more than we need to chase Kirdash."

I wasn't sure I was right. Now that the battle was over, I was mostly relieved we'd survived. I went to the unconscious soldiers who had been injured.

The major looked worried, but it didn't appear as if anyone was dead. If I had anything to do with it, no one *would* die, either. I knelt by the unconscious soldiers, two of whom had taken the brunt of the explosion Kirdash had caused.

Reaching into their bodies, I located the broken parts and bleeding areas, noting they had swelling in the brain as well. Using the energy in the crystals I wore, I repaired everything that seemed dangerous, being extra careful with their brains as I reduced the swelling and repaired the blood vessels.

Neither woke up, but their bodies relaxed, their breathing slowed, and their faces looked more peaceful.

When I was sure they were out of the woods and their bodies could handle the rest, I let go and moved on. There were eight more soldiers, three centaurs, and five elves with injuries. Some of the elves aided me, and I worried about them the least since our bodies were good at healing.

The humans needed all the help they could get, however, and I repaired some broken bones and torn ligaments as well as fixing gaping wounds while everyone else watched. Then I moved to the few dark elves who had been captured or had surrendered.

None of them spoke as I healed them, fixing anything that was life-threatening or causing great pain but leaving the bruises and scrapes.

When the last of them was out of pain, I noticed that a calm quiet had settled over the group. Everyone was resting or going about some minor task. Even the mythicals we'd captured for their own good were peaceful.

I stood up as Minsheng came over and put a hand on my shoulder.

"You've grown so much in a short space of time. Let's finish what we've started."

Grinning, I nodded, then pulled the candy bar I could see out of his top pocket.

"I'm going to need to recharge," I said as I unwrapped it and took a bite.

Minsheng laughed.

"I've been feeding you since the moment I set eyes on you. I can do so a few more times."

This had everyone laughing, and the laughter got through to the soldiers I'd left unconscious. They opened their eyes, then blinked. Not enjoying being in the limelight, I pulled back and went over to Nerik.

The dragon was still resting.

"You expended a lot of energy healing them," he said, his voice low so only I'd hear.

"They needed it, especially the human soldiers. They came to rescue friends of mine. No one willing to risk their life for another should lose it if something can be done. I figured the dark elves follow Kirdash because they fear him. If you give people hope, often they make different choices."

"That's not the attitude the old elves had."

"I'm not one of the old elves. I'm a mix of everything: elf, dragon, gnome, human. I'm all of us."

"You're Henera." The dragon lowered his head. "I'll serve your cause until this land is free."

"Thank you," I replied, the weight of what I was being offered not lost on me.

"No, it is I who should thank you. When Kirdash entered my mind and forced a bond upon me, I felt the pain and fear every mythical he has enslaved for generations has felt. I was blind to it, but you didn't hesitate to free me. My ancestors and I should be ashamed that we've hidden from the fight for so long."

"Maybe that is true and maybe it isn't, but you can't change any of it now. All you can do is make the best decision at each moment going forward."

"In that case, Henera, let me fly you to yonder compound to get your mythicals back."

I grinned as he hunkered down to make it easier for me to climb onto his back. Within seconds, we were in the air and on our way to the compound.

My army had grown. Everyone was tired and running on less magic, but several of the dark elves had asked to join us now that they were healed. I had no objection, and neither did anyone else. All of us had been enemies in the past, but we had become allies and fought side by side against a bigger threat.

I looked at the palace as we neared it. The building was impressive and foreboding, but it held something I wanted beyond anything else. Although I couldn't be sure what we'd face, and I was drained to some degree, Kirdash had fled, and the dark elves we'd faced and beaten had come from here.

There was a good chance the building ahead was no

longer well-guarded, and I planned to make it clear that whoever guarded it could not stand against me.

I spotted dark elves on the battlements and in the windows of the towers. It was clear they were watching us. They had seen the battle, so they were aware that I had bested Kirdash in combat as well as turned some of their allies to my side.

"Swoop over them low and slow if you can do so without getting hurt," I said to Nerik. As we got even closer, more dark elves appeared, brandishing weapons and donning armor.

The dragon swept around one end of the palace so he could fly me over it.

"I don't want to fight any of you," I projected as he brought me overhead. "None of you have any reason to fear me, but I do have the power to take this building by force if necessary."

I paused since Nerik had to bank and come back around to give me the distance I needed.

"Kirdash fled, but I know he holds many mythicals here. I'm looking for four he stole from me and others from allies of mine. Turn them over, and I will leave you to do as you wish."

"The Henera doesn't flee," someone yelled. I couldn't see who it was.

"Did you not witness the battle? Can you not see the elves of your kind coming up the road toward you, healed and well. Does that not speak for itself? My words might not sway you, but what do my actions say? What do the actions of Kirdash tell you?"

There was no response to my words at first. Nerik kept circling, out of reach of any weapon or magic that might be used against me, while the dark elves wearing the most ornate armor had a brief conversation. They came to an agreement, and one of them stepped forward, his eyes on me.

Nerik brought me closer without me needing to ask him to, then he slowly beat his wings, hovering.

"We will meet with you and the dark elves who return with you and see the truth of your words for ourselves."

"So be it, but know this. Any treachery will be met with force. I will defend those I care about."

This gained me a bow, then the dark elves swept toward a set of stairs.

Slowly Nerik landed in front of the main gate, and my army came to join us, walking up at a gentle pace to stand beside me.

By the time they arrived, the gates were swinging open, then a troop of dark elves came out. There were less than thirty of them, but they were armored, and several wore gauntlets and other accessories that appeared to hold elemental power.

If my group had been fresh, we could have taken these dark elves on and made short work of the palace guard. In our present state, I wasn't as sure, but I had no intention of betraying that emotion to the guards.

The one in charge came and surveyed the dark elves with me. I motioned for them to come closer.

They conversed among themselves for a short while, and I hung back to give them the privacy to do so. Although I tried to appear calm and as if this didn't bother me or impact me in any way, I didn't succeed as well this time.

These dark elves were deciding if I was going to get easy access to the mythicals they held, and I could do nothing but wait.

CHAPTER TWENTY-SEVEN

The dark elves finished their conversation. The general came toward me, no fear or aggression in his stance.

"I won't pretend to understand who you are and what you are capable of, but you show more mercy and heart than we are used to from your kind." His voice was deep but even and measured, as if he'd thought carefully about what he was saying.

"Thank you. I don't know what has happened between my kind and yours in the past. All I know is that Kirdash stole my bonded mythicals, and they'll be hurting without me."

"We are willing to trust you to some degree, but I would like to see what the mythicals choose for themselves. If they are here as you believe and choose you and those with you, you may take them. Can you agree to that?"

"Completely. Their freedom to choose and live a free life along with all the mythicals I protect is all I've ever wanted." I sighed, my relief apparent.

The dark elf nodded again, giving me a bow. Then he backed up and made it clear I could enter the palace.

I had expected none of this, but I wasn't going to say no to an easier option that reduced the chances of anyone getting hurt and saved me magic. My army moved to come with me, but I held up my hand to stop them so we didn't make these dark elves feel threatened.

"You shouldn't go in there alone," Minsheng stated, coming close as if to plead with me.

"You do not have to come alone," the dark elf added, seeing the exchange for what it was: concern for my safety.

I stopped and thought. It made sense to bring some of my army with me, but I didn't want to leave them vulnerable, either. The elves who had lost their bonded mythicals came forward, making the decision for me.

Of all my allies, these had the most to gain from going inside. They were also the most powerful. It solved the problem nicely. It was a small group, but in truth, I was bringing about half the power of the army with me.

The dark elf waved us through and stepped back to give us the space we needed. It was late in the day, but the palace was still bright inside, the large windows and the decor making it seem stunning.

It didn't look like a prison, but it was. The mythicals were trapped somewhere in here.

Before anyone could show me where to go, I heard a familiar roar, this time pained. Zephyr was here.

"Zephyr?" I yelled, using the air to carry my voice to wherever he was.

"Aella?" his voice came back.

I ran through hallways and corridors as he called to me

from somewhere deeper in the palace. Everyone followed, and the guards bristled as if they thought I was going to attack, but someone shouted for them to let me through, and they obeyed.

It didn't take long to find the large room where Zephyr was being held. The large bronze dragon took up most of it, no room for him to stretch his wings. A net stretched across his back, restraining him, and a dark elf stood nearby with a weapon in his hands.

"Let him go," I said, the words coming out low and menacing as I went to Zephyr's head and reached up for him.

No one moved, just stared at Zephyr and me. My dragon lowered his head and rested it on mine, the relief in his body evident.

"Don't make me say it again." I looked at the nearest dark elf.

The captor hesitated, looking at the general who had arrived seconds after me. I glared at the dark elf, fearing he wasn't going to keep his end of the bargain.

"Do you want to go with her, dragon?"

"Of course, you imbecile. She's the Henera and was my bonded before Kirdash stole me." Zephyr's words were full of anger, no hint of pain in them now, to my relief.

"Then you are free to go."

I exhaled and used my abilities to unclasp the net pinning him in place before anyone else could move.

"Where are the others?" I asked as I leaned into Zephyr again, feeling his smooth, warm scales beneath my fingers. Tears threatened to fall. Their cause? Being close to the dragon I feared I might never see again.

"More creatures came in at the same time as this drag-on," the dark elf said.

"Three more of them are mine, and the rest likely belong to the elves with me," I replied as Zephyr shook off the last of the net and stretched.

The dark elf's mouth fell open.

"You have more than one bond?"

"I did have and I will again, but only the four who came to me naturally. I won't force my bond upon any others."

This made the general nod and bow again, sweeping low as he motioned for us to follow him. The double doors at the end of the room were flung open. They were barely big enough for Zephyr to fit through, but he wriggled until he made it, then we were in a courtyard.

I found Roth, Sen, and Nuri out there in cages, none of them big enough. Seth's fire fox and Cherisse's otter-like creature were out here as well.

We all ran to our mythicals and freed them. Tears flowed even more freely.

Sen bounded onto one shoulder to cuddle my neck, and Nuri landed on the other side. I stumbled, the relief making it hard to do anything but weep with joy. Despite being with them, I couldn't feel them in my head, and I wasn't sure how to re-bond with them.

All five of us came together, the mythicals reaching for each other too—all of us one big family. I tried not to worry about it. We could figure that part out.

Closing my eyes, I reached out to find Kirdash's bonds, but I couldn't feel anything but them. Then there were four flashes of light, one right after the other.

A rush of emotions, pictures, and words flooded my

mind, and I fell to my knees. Zephyr and Roth lowered their heads. I sent warmth to all of them, the love I felt at that moment overwhelming. Joy went with it. My delight in being close to them and bonded again made my heart soar.

I was even more powerful, the bonds giving me a strength I hadn't realized was gone until it came back.

We finally calmed down, and I got to my feet. The entire time, the dark elves had looked on. Cherisse, Seth, and Serfina had re-bonded with their mythicals, making it clear that all of us were wanted by the creatures we had come for.

"It is clear these creatures would prefer to be yours." The general came closer.

"Will you let the rest of the mythicals in here go as well?" I asked. "I don't know how many you have, but I'm certain they were all taken the same way. They should bond with those of their choosing."

"While I don't think I have the power to stop you from taking what you wish, I cannot place the dark elves here in danger by defying our leader to that extent."

"Then don't stay here. We will return to Earth through the portals, then we will find Kirdash and challenge him to let you all go and stop this madness. You won't ever see him again."

Silence met my words, the dark elves not knowing how to take this.

"I won't force you to do anything. I came here to free all the creatures who were kept against their will. Mine or not, it's clear that none of them want to be here. Will you not let them go?"

Before the general could reply, one of the dark elves near a cage containing several birds opened the door, then stood back. Several more guards moved to the nearest cage or contraption restraining a mythical and freed them.

There were roars, squawks, and other noises of gratitude, many of the mythical creatures understanding enough to know they had been freed and their ordeal was over. Few of them went far, the courtyard being in the middle of a large building, but it was done.

The general deflated but accepted his subordinates' actions without reprimand.

"I'm going now. Any mythicals who wish to come with me are welcome. There is a Sanctuary city on Earth where many creatures and elves reside together in harmony."

The dark elves stood to the side, but they needn't have bothered. I wasn't going back through the main doors.

Moving to Zephyr, I asked if he would bear my weight.

Always, he replied, his voice sounding in my head for the first time in days.

I climbed onto his back and settled into a position that felt right. He didn't hesitate to fly upward. Roth and Nuri did the same, and Sen tucked herself into my neck and nuzzled me again.

Using my abilities, I gently lifted the creatures who couldn't fly over to the army waiting on the other side.

When the mythical creatures saw the people who had come to rescue them, there were more noises of delight and happiness. They were met with shouts and cheers.

Zephyr swooped in and landed in front of them, and the large gold dragon who had been circling also touched down. I marveled at seeing the dragons side by side, inclining their heads to each other respectfully.

"I've felt some of the pain you must have felt," Nerik told Zephyr. "I'm glad we found you and spared you more."

"Thank you for bearing Aella when I could not," Zephyr replied. "Consider your debt to the ancients repaid."

I lifted an eyebrow, not sure what this meant. Although his words made the gold dragon look happier, he shook his head.

"My conscience will not allow an easy settlement. There are more places such as this one with creatures enslaved and trapped and many more military-style buildings full of dark elves and slaves. Enough is enough. Everyone should be free, and the planet should be allowed to recover and grow once more."

I wasn't going to argue.

"Once we've found Kirdash and stopped him, we'll come back and help," I assured him. "Give everyone what they need."

The golden dragon swept his head down again before flying back to his mountain. Without another word, everyone else headed out too. It wasn't ideal, the trek having taken us several days, but there was one way back, and I wouldn't leave anyone behind.

Some of the mythicals flashed with light as they came closer to the elves with our group, and there were squeals and yells of delight as pairs bonded for the first time, as they had when we'd freed the first compound of mythical creatures. It made my heart even lighter and gave everyone an emotional boost for the return journey.

Despite the success of our mission and the warmth and

joy of having my mythicals back, I couldn't relax. Kirdash was out there somewhere, and he wasn't going to be happy about what had happened. His forces were formidable, even if they were spread out.

I wanted to get everyone to safety before he could come back with an even bigger army.

I don't think he'll come back in a hurry, Zephyr said, the reassurance in his voice something I'd missed. *You trounced him...without all of us.*

Zephyr had a point. There were a lot more mythicals with us now, and we had gained some dark elves too; the ones who had been captured and healed were still marching along beside us. We weren't weak.

Despite that, I considered the other portal option that had been mentioned. I wasn't sure it was a good idea to open more of them, but I'd stood against Kirdash in battle and fared far better than the first time.

I would face him once more, however. I had a feeling it wouldn't be long before we clashed again.

CHAPTER TWENTY-EIGHT

We traveled for over a day before there was any sign of anyone else, our food supply dropping lower than I'd have liked with so many extra mouths to feed. I'd called a halt for the water elves to bring up the life-giving liquid from a well we found along the way and pass it out when there was movement to the east.

Zephyr came to my side, and Nuri shot into the air to get a closer look from above.

None of my mythicals had ventured very far from me since we'd reunited, and our bond tugged as the firebird flew away. I had to resist the urge to call him back.

He projected what he could see: my friends hurrying along toward us. It was Simon, with a small group of powerful elves.

I rushed toward them, not sure what could have brought them into such a dangerous place unless it was urgent and they needed me.

"There you are," Simon said as he slowed. He looked

exhausted, his air powers having been tapped to move them at speed.

"Come and rest and tell me everything," I said as I merged my control with his and took over, giving them a boost with my mind that would ease their travels without taxing them.

"There's no time. We've opened another portal to get you off this planet. Kirdash attacked. The dark elf is on Earth, and we can't hold him back much longer."

I growled. Although I had suspected that he was up to something, I hadn't thought about him going to Earth. It made sense. I couldn't stop him if I was on his planet doing something else.

"How far is it to the portal?" I asked as Zephyr rushed back to the group to tell them the news and hurry them along with whatever they needed.

"About three hours at the pace we came here, but I don't have the strength or ability to get back so fast."

I put my hand on Simon's shoulder, calming him.

"We'll get back," I said, my stomach knotting with fear despite the confidence in my voice and appearance. "Which portal is he attacking on Earth?"

"Most of them," Simon replied. "But he's at the Californian one."

"The ones in Greenland and Ireland too?"

"Greenland, yes. Ireland, no," he replied as the rest of the army joined us. Everything was packed. Minsheng handed me a full canteen.

I gratefully drank some water as we started to march to the new portal. Simon told me everything he knew and related how he'd got to us so fast.

The knowledge that they'd opened another portal so swiftly worried me. I had a lot of the powerful elves with me and many of the tablets and crystals, but I'd left enough behind that they could break the pillars around another and open it as a group, merging many minds to get the job done.

"The elves were managing to keep the dark elf underground and buried when I left, but they can't hold out against him forever." Simon looked at me with hope in his eyes.

"If I can get there, I can stop him," I replied. I wanted to believe my words, but I was drained. If he had a large army with him, it would be one very tough fight.

It all depended on what he had with him. The truth was, I had no idea.

Onward we marched. Everyone merged their minds with mine. Although we'd need power for the fight, the sooner we got there, the easier it would be to push Kirdash back and keep him from getting loose and his army from hurting people.

Time went by in a blur, earth elementals straightening and flattening paths and getting us to our destination while air elementals powered us on faster, the wind always at our backs. The water elementals kept us hydrated along the way and the weather from turning on us, and the fire elementals kept us warm enough as night fell and the air got colder.

It all helped, and I believed we would succeed, but there was still a lot to be done. The portal on the other side was a fair distance from the portal in California. There was a plane waiting to get all of us into battle fast. The US military was going to be there too.

Whatever happened, I wouldn't be alone.

The portal stood in another derelict building, something no one would have thought contained anything of note. I felt better about it being open.

Sierrathen stood by it, concern on her face as she wrung her hands together. I wasn't sure why she had stayed until I saw the canteens of water she'd prepared. She'd known we'd be coming in exhausted and would need to recover. A soldier hung back in the shadows behind her, holding a gun and generally looking fierce.

I smiled at seeing humans and elves working together, one there to protect the other if the worst happened.

When I came up to her, I grabbed a drink and noticed there were also snack bars.

"There's more food and drink on the planes," Sierrathen told me. "And we've got food, bedding, and crates for the mythical creatures in another to take any that need healing straight to the Sanctuary."

I quickly filled her in on the state of things and what had happened, gratitude rushing through me as Gwaelon came to the front and organized the mythicals while I went to the soldier.

"Kirdash hadn't broken through half an hour ago, ma'am," the soldier said without me needing to ask. He wasn't afraid of saying the dark elf's name, as many others were. "But our forces are hard-pressed at every location. None have been able to get to the Californian portal to aid them."

"Can the others hold?"

"We could divert more soldiers to them if we knew you were heading out to defeat the dark elf."

"I beat him once recently. I'll beat him again." I hoped that saying it often enough would make it true.

It wasn't arrogance as much as need. I didn't have a choice. If the two planets were to be saved, I had to defeat him, and I couldn't fall in battle again.

Without waiting for more information, I gestured for anyone fit to fight to fly out with me. Zephyr had to take human form to get through the building's door.

The minutes it took to travel between the worlds felt like an age this time. I was thinking about all the ways that Kirdash could break through the defenses and how quickly he could kill people I cared about if he got the chance. I could get there far too late.

To my surprise, Nerik was on the other side. He was in dragon form and had elves I didn't recognize with him, as well as some of the dwarves and gnomes from his settlement.

"Don't look so surprised to see me," he greeted me. "I told you I would fight with you. I flew home to get those who could help. We've modified the planes and have more crystals. My elves aren't fighters, but they've given you and the other elves energy to use in battle."

I nodded, gratitude sweeping through me as he slipped yet another bracelet on my wrist and held out more badge-like artifacts with crystals in them.

They held a lot of raw power, and it made me wonder how many days the dragon had been filling them. Had he intended to help me for longer than he'd let on, or had these energy crystals been made for a different purpose?

I didn't know, and it wasn't the time to ask, but there were lots more water crystals than other colors.

"Can we put some of these on my mythicals?" I asked, but again the dragon beat me to it.

His dwarves had designed and made something for each of them to replace what Kirdash had taken, Roth getting a crystal added to each of his hooves and another to work with the device that concentrated the jet of water from his head.

I grinned as a small crystal was fitted to a new suit of golden scale armor for Sen and placed on her. Nuri had a necklace slipped over his head, part of it trailing his chest and connecting to his legs so it wouldn't fall off if he flew upside-down.

Then the dragon presented Zephyr with another circlet, his original one nowhere to be found.

"You look better with this than the rest of us," Nerik told him.

It was all we had time for since the nearest soldier's radio crackled to life with reports of Kirdash almost breaking through the defenses at the portal site.

"Get me there as quickly as you can," I said and ushered everyone with me toward the plane at a sprint.

Fear rippled through me. I trusted our allies to do their job, but I sat inside the plane and reached for the air around us. I let most of it flow as it naturally would, but I aided my allies in moving faster to get them inside the aircraft.

When we were in the air, three planes flying together, I used my abilities to tweak airflow and control gusts of wind and the weather around us to make conditions as favorable as possible. We needed to get into this fight.

Despite my best efforts, we were hours away. Who knew how long the elves could hold out?

I listened to the reports from the ground as they came into the cockpit and experienced relief as each half-hour brought no change. The elves and soldiers were holding for now. The earth elves were draining themselves but were tiring the dark elves trapped underground at a similar rate.

For a short while, I had the relief of knowing that Kirdash had returned to his planet, not drained but retreating for some reason. It was short-lived, however. Half an hour later, the dark elf had returned, and he came back with renewed strength.

The final report we got, fifteen minutes before we were due to arrive, sent a chill through me. Kirdash had broken through, suddenly significantly more powerful, and the earth elves were collectively not enough to prevent him from tunneling out.

I heard gunshots in the background of the radio message. The soldiers holding the portal were firing. With all the power Kirdash possessed, I wasn't sure what good it would do, so we had to get going. Despite the plane being fast, it wasn't faster than a flying dragon.

Time for us to go, I told my bonded mythicals, but I needn't have bothered.

They were on their feet, and Minsheng had my pack for me. "We'll catch up. Go kick some ass."

Feeling like I would throw up with fear and pumped

with adrenaline at getting to do something I'd done many times before, I moved to the back of the plane as a soldier hit the button to open the hatch. There were so many mythicals on the plane that Zephyr wasn't in dragon form, so he needed to turn into a dragon as soon as he was outside.

Sen tucked herself into my jacket. Nuri and Roth were on one side of me, and Zephyr was on the other. We wore every crystal we had, the power making them glow. As one, we jumped and flew toward the battle.

Zephyr transformed before my eyes and spread his wings. He fell, but it didn't take long for him to recover, then he came up below me. The two of us came together as we had done many times before.

Other mythicals who could fly and air elves came out of the plane after us, some bearing other elves or bonded mythicals. I didn't have time to wait for them, however.

Below and ahead, I could see the battle raging as dark elves came spilling out of the underground building with the portal inside. Our elves had fallen back to a barrier they'd created since the last time I was there and the soldiers were tucked in with them, doing their best to fight back.

Now that the dam had burst, however, so many dark elves poured out that I could see the defenders were overwhelmed. I couldn't see Kirdash anywhere.

Trying not to panic, I helped Zephyr and my mythicals fly faster, tapping into the air crystals dotted all over my body. We powered closer, and shouts went up when we and the reinforcements behind us were spotted.

I didn't wait to land to begin working out where to hit

the dark elves. We aimed to touch down in front of the defenders, and I threw up an air barrier ahead of us.

As we landed, I flew off Zephyr's back. He transformed in mid-air, grabbing the earth and making barriers of vines that sprouted and traveled at speed toward the enemy. Sen bounded out of my jacket and onto Roth's back, from which she fired ice darts. He shot jets of water. Nuri became a ball of fire hurtling toward the enemy, and I hit them with air blasts from my gloves.

Within seconds, we'd changed the shape of the battle. The elves and the soldiers behind us cheered, calling "Hen-era" louder than ever.

We had a reprieve, but I could feel the forces and power coming. Kirdash was here. I didn't need to see him to feel that he had gained aid and more crystals, as I had done.

The dark elf finally stepped out of the building and into the light. Every eye turned to him.

"Hello, my dear," he said, projecting his voice so everyone would hear it despite it being directed at me. "Shall we dance?"

CHAPTER TWENTY-NINE

Kirdash didn't wait for me to reply. His mind latched onto mine as he blasted air, earth, heat, and water outward in an arc.

Managing to block the elemental part of the attack, I kept everyone safe behind me, but his mind locked on, and he pushed his way into my head.

It's over, I thought before he could mock or gloat. *I will beat you today.*

As always, he laughed, but it wasn't the assured laugh it had been in the past. I'd beaten him before and although his defeat of me had given me a reason to doubt, so had my subsequent defeat of him. The truth was, we had each won once in the past. There was no way to know who would win this.

I attacked his mind, feeling him trying to break the new bonds. Nuri coached me through it as he dove toward some dark elves who were edging to one side of the battle-field to come around from behind.

Roth blasted water at the entrance of the building,

sending the emerging dark elves reeling before they could get out. Emily and Simon landed together, then aided Roth and Emily's mythical to draw up more water and hurl it.

More elves landed around me as I took several steps forward. With the gap closing between the forces, the elemental attacks became more brutal, faster, and more furious.

Several hit me, and I staggered under their force as well as Kirdash's mind. He grinned and doubled his efforts, tapping into the crystals he wore.

Patience, Zephyr said as I went to connect to more of my crystals and draw on their power. *The only way to defeat Kirdash is to drain him of his power. We need to be smarter.*

We need to dance, I replied, grinning.

Dance with the elements and protect our people. More help is on the way, and our soldiers will still be shooting long after every elf and dark elf is drained.

It was a good strategy and a reminder that Zephyr had the memories of the ancient line of dragons to draw on. I couldn't begin to describe how much I'd missed his wisdom in my head, but I intended to put it to good use.

I put some distance between Kirdash and us and stopped attacking his mind to defend my own. I broke his grip each time he reached for us, protecting my mythicals from being taken.

The tactic wasn't easy. It was like he understood what we were doing or thought I was tired, so he continued to press and push to get into my head. I kept putting distance between us, moving around the battlefield, turning the tide in smaller battles, and pushing back or incapacitating a dark elf here and there.

It wasn't long before even more reinforcements arrived, more soldiers and Nerik joining the fight. The gold dragon flew overhead. More dark elves poured out of the building as the entire mountain was reformed by the earth elementals coming through the portal.

Before long, the portal was exposed. The building was gone, melted into the earth around it. Elves fought behind air barriers against dark elves in armor, and the soldiers did their best to pick off targets.

Mythicals ran, jumped, and flew around us, some controlled by Kirdash and the rest bonded to elves. I broke Kirdash's connection as he stole someone's mythical. Once or twice he succeeded, but I pushed him back and broke his new bond.

Using my link with Zephyr, we concentrated on getting the soldiers to target the mythicals controlled by Kirdash and hit them with tranquilizers. That infuriated him, and he redoubled his assault on my mind.

I had to step back to break his grasp while using an air barrier to keep a water blast from knocking me off my feet. Roth darted across the water beam, absorbing it and using it on two earth elves who were building a structure to hide behind. The water washed them and their construction away.

Trying not to let Kirdash in, I ducked behind Cherisse as she stepped over to control the water with the otter on her shoulder. I leaped onto Roth, then toward the water elementals attacking us.

No longer needing to win that fight, I launched into the air and over to some dark elves who were setting fire to one of our earth elementals' plants. I stole the heat, then regrew the vines for the earth elemental in control of them.

Another little battle having turned in our favor, I moved on again. Kirdash followed, also flying above the crowds. His mind hit mine with so much power that he breached my defenses.

I almost fell out of the sky, reeling in pain and shock, but I held on and turned to face him. This didn't seem to be working. He wasn't getting drained quickly enough, and he wasn't giving me enough space to work. I somehow had to hold out, though.

We flew above the battlefield, getting higher as I blasted him with air to keep him at a distance. He laughed in my head.

You don't seem as calm, my dear. Not enjoying this dance?

It's okay, Aella, Nuri said, his words soothing me. *You know what to do. You just have to keep doing it.*

Kirdash's gaze flicked to the firebird. Nuri dove over two water elves so close that the water they controlled boiled and steamed, then Emily blasted it at them.

Seeing one of my mythicals get the better of the dark elves made me calm down and refocus. Nuri had walked me through this many times. I just had to keep doing it, as he said. Keep protecting my mythicals. We had to hold this battle line long enough for the dark elves to drain themselves.

As I broke the connection again, I maneuvered, dancing around him. It wasn't ideal, but it was all I had to work with, elaborately flying through the air.

This was where I was most comfortable. I'd been fighting in the air for years.

Kirdash had more power in his crystals than I did. Mine were running low, the circlet and one of the bracelets I wore having been drained during our previous fight and not replenished.

We need to steal his crystals, Zephyr suggested.

How are we going to do that?

Sen do it. Sen good at getting small things. I could hear the delight in her voice at the idea, and it took all my control not to refuse it as being unsafe. Kirdash could crush her.

We'll need to get him on the ground, I mused, pondering how Sen might go about it.

And we'll need to distract him, so he doesn't notice Sen taking them, Zephyr added.

I frowned, not sure how we'd manage the last part but determined to try. Nerik swooped overhead again, noticing that I was backing up and dancing to the sides, staying at the current range and keeping Kirdash at bay.

The large gold dragon exhaled his breath weapon and coated the area in white. I took control of it, and Kirdash tried to steal it from me a second later. I moved it over some dark elves, and not all of them had the sense to hold their breath.

Several of them collapsed, paralyzed, and I heard Kirdash growl in frustration. I also noticed that the dark elves who had been pouring through the portal were no longer an endless force rushing in. They had hunkered down, and the portal was merely the beacon behind enemy lines that we were aiming for.

Although I tried to bring the gas up and wrap it around Kirdash, he was also holding an air barrier around him. It kept the vapor from getting too close to him. He was also good at swirling the wind to tear the cloud apart and make it too thin to be of use.

I let it go when it became apparent that it wasn't going to take anyone else out of the fight. I needed to get Kirdash to go lower. I tried to lift and push him with air, but he danced as well as I did, so I had to head back toward the ground. That didn't work either. Kirdash appeared determined to stay in the air.

When Nerik swept overhead again, he flew lower, encouraging Kirdash down by attempting to rake his claws across his chest. The dark elf did retreat downward, but only for a second. Then he rose again and focused on Nerik.

A moment later, Nerik roared as Kirdash switched his mental target from me to the dragon and forced a bond on him.

Pissed on Nerik's behalf and worried as well, I reached out to Kirdash's mind as he often did mine and attempted to pull control of Nerik away from him.

It took some time, given the extra crystals Kirdash had powering his mind and defenses, but I managed to push through when Zephyr merged his mind with mine and bolstered my attack.

I quickly broke the bond, freeing the dragon and the other mythicals. That made Kirdash growl again, but he didn't return his attention to me. Instead, he focused on the dragon again.

Without being bonded to him, there wasn't a lot I could do to defend the dragon from the attack, however. This was confirmed when Kirdash repeated the forced bond and the dragon roared in pain.

Can you bond with him? Zephyr asked.

I hesitated. *Could I? Would that work?*

Kirdash has lots of bonds, Zephyr added.

But all of his are forced and painful for the mythical.

Only because we fight it.

It was a good point, and it made me consider it. I couldn't keep trading blows with Kirdash over the dragon. It would tire me out fast, and I had no idea if it was even difficult for the dark elf.

Once again, I latched onto his mind and felt for the bonds he'd established. He fought me harder this time, but with Zephyr aiding me and all the crystals we had, we broke the bond. This time, however, I reached for the dragon's mind, not pushing hard but suggesting a connection.

While I was doing that, I flew up and closer to the dragon, wanting to give Nerik some idea of what I was doing as I did it. I didn't have to get very close for there to be a brilliant flash of light, and then I could feel Nerik in my mind.

There were gasps and shouts from beneath us, and the battle cry "Henera" that everyone had shouted when I arrived was repeated.

Thank you, Nerik said, his voice loud and clear. *I'm not sure I could have handled Kirdash taking control of me a fourth time.*

I can't promise he won't, I replied as the dark elf yelled in rage and tried to latch onto my mind again. This time Nerik helped me fight the attack, diving at the dark elf while I danced to one side and down.

Nerik took Kirdash by surprise, and one of his claws got through the barrier and opened a cut across the dark elf's shoulder and arm. While it wasn't deep and would only leave a faint scar, it distracted Kirdash enough that I could brush off his mind.

Now we needed to get him on the ground or close enough that Sen could jump up. But the dark elf's rage grew. He bellowed at the dragon and flew after Nerik.

I tried to follow, but there was little I could do. Nerik banked again, and Kirdash pulled something out of his jacket. A blade glinted in the sun, then Kirdash flew as fast as I could and drove the weapon through a gap in the softer scales covering the dragon's underbelly.

Pain tore through me and the rest of my mythicals as Kirdash delivered a fatal blow to the dragon. Nerik fell out of the sky. I fell as well, and Zephyr and Nuri did too.

Air caught me, controlled by someone else, but I was soon able to use it to slow Nerik's descent and catch everyone else. Kirdash didn't stop there, however. He flew at Nerik again, forcing me to intercept.

I flew straight at Kirdash and grabbed at the wrist holding the blade. He was strong, and it felt strange to touch him when I had been keeping away.

I held on as he wriggled and pulled away, my martial arts training lending me an advantage. It took me a moment, but I managed to find an opening to disarm him. I grabbed the blade and flew toward Nerik.

As I reached the large golden dragon's side, I realized the blade I was holding had an array of crystals in the hilt, and it was brimming with power.

There were more built into the internals of the dagger that powered something the blade did, but I didn't have time to find out what. I landed beside Nerik and rushed to his side to heal him.

Kirdash flew at me to take the weapon back. He knocked me over before I could brace myself, but I bounced back up to stab him. I missed when he used the air to dodge, and the barrier around him made it harder for me to reach his body.

I tapped into the crystals it carried to speed up my body and form a stronger barrier around me as I blocked another direct attack.

Kirdash pulled another knife from his jacket, and the two of us danced around each other in a new way. I parried and dodged, trying to find or create an opening while we moved far faster than humanly possible.

Pain lanced my arm as he caught me, the blow light enough that it drew a thin red line and stung but wasn't dangerous.

The pain distracted my other mythicals again and made me realize I couldn't feel any pain from Nerik anymore. I wanted to check that the dragon was okay, but I couldn't, locked in battle as I was and having to concentrate on making sure Kirdash didn't run me through.

While we fought, Sen ran up. I saw her bound onto the back of the dark elf's cloak and lunged to distract him from the weight she'd have added. By making my move too soon, I opened myself up to attack, and Kirdash took the opportunity.

His blade found my flesh once more, catching me by a rib on my right-hand side. The pain was intense and made me squeal and back off from the fight a moment.

"Not dancing so well now, my dear."

I tried not to rise to the bait as Zephyr ran in, the vine-whip knife in his hands. He distracted Kirdash by attacking him as I reached into my body and healed myself. As soon as the pain had eased, I rejoined the fray, and Kirdash faced the two of us.

The dark elf snarled and focused his attacks on Zephyr, but the dragon had trained in fighting with me, and we could also read each other's minds. We danced around Kirdash as the dark elf grew weary, panting when he would normally have been fine.

He flew up and away from us a moment later, fleeing. Sen dropped to the ground, clutching four crystals.

She ran off, and Kirdash tried to fly away, but his power had decreased. Along with Zephyr, I took control of the air around Kirdash and forced him to the ground again. He hit hard but fought back, striking at my mind.

I blocked him, drawing on the crystals I carried. Once more, he grabbed the air and ran away. We pushed him down again, and someone raised an earth barrier in front of him and in a circle around us, boxing him in with Zephyr and me.

I put an air barrier over the top. Simon's mind and control merged with mine, all his remaining power going into holding it with me.

Kirdash snarled as he rounded on me, still clutching the weapon.

"I don't suppose you'd surrender if I asked you to?" I inquired. I was not sure I wanted to kill the dark elf, even after all he'd done.

"And let myself be caged again? I'd rather bleed out here and now."

"That can be arranged," Zephyr replied.

Although the anger in Zephyr's voice surprised me, I agreed, and we ran toward the dark elf.

As we closed the gap, I blasted air at the blade Kirdash held to push it away. The dark elf held me off, and once again, the three of us danced. Our blades moved faster than the eye could follow, muscle memory keeping the pair of us from being impaled.

This time I was the first to score a hit, my blade cutting deep into Kirdash's arm. He bellowed but thrust back. Zephyr blocked, saving me from being sliced again.

I danced back, knowing we had the upper hand. The dark elf would tire long before we did. He rushed in, not giving me a reprieve, but Zephyr got in the way again. The extra speed cost the dark elf; a crystal around his neck went dark.

Sensing our advantage, I hit him with an air blast and pushed him back, using air to hold him in one place. He fought my mind and kept the air barrier around him, but it slipped.

Not waiting for him to recover, I formed a tight box around his head. Zephyr used earth and vines to trap Kirdash's limbs and hold him still. The dark elf fought, his other crystals boosting the earth element, but more minds merged with ours since the battle had ended outside our enclosure.

I stepped closer again, drawing on everything I had to close the air barrier around Kirdash's head and pull out the air. He fought me when he sensed what I was doing. I wanted to stop when I saw the fear in his eyes, but this elf had caused much devastation and destruction.

"Surrender," I demanded.

"No," he replied, using up some of his precious air.

Without warning, he lashed out again, connecting with my mind. He tried to claw my bonds away from me and sent waves of pain my way, the link between us acting like my bonds with my mythicals.

I almost let go of everything as his images and memories flooded my mind, sick thoughts of what he wanted to do to me added in. My stomach churned, but Nuri flew onto my shoulder, and Zephyr put his arm around me and sent waves of love, calm, and hope at me.

Roth rushed up, the pegasus nuzzling me from the other side, then Sen bounded onto my other shoulder.

Break his attacks as you've always done, Henera, Nuri said as Sen leaped onto Kirdash where he couldn't reach her and stripped more crystals off his body.

I refocused, tightening the air around the dark elf's head and reaching around the mental connection to break the link from the side. It took more concentration than normal since my abilities were also drained. Eventually it snapped, however, and he was gone again.

Seconds later, Kirdash struggled to take his last breath. I kept the box around his head, staring at him as he stopped moving and closed his eyes. I reached into his body, feeling his mind trying to heal the damage and repair everything, drawing in air from other places.

I fought the control there too, remembering what I'd been told about his ability to keep himself alive as long as his powers held out. Not long after, Sen finished stripping his body of crystals and brought them all to me, dropping them into one hand.

Melding all their power into mine, I held on until Kirdash's heart stopped beating and his mind and powers no longer pushed against my control. As I stared at his peaceful-looking face, I realized I was crying.

Zephyr gently pulled me away.

"It's done," he said. "You stopped him, and both worlds are safe now."

I wasn't sure I believed him, but I let go and allowed Zephyr to pull me away. Then I remembered Nerik. I rushed toward the large dragon as Zephyr and others brought down the wall we'd created.

Nerik wasn't breathing either, but several of the healer elves ran up as I jogged closer, all of us merging minds and reaching into the large scaled body.

The destruction the blade had done inside of the dragon was immense, and I didn't need to feel it for long to know we were far too late. The elemental blade had torn organs apart and set off an explosion that reacted with the paralyzing gas internally.

I'd been crying, but the tears flowed even faster now. Although I hadn't known the dragon well, I knew what he represented and that he'd given his life to aid us. I felt a similar pain in Zephyr's chest as he looked at the dead form of the only other member of his species he'd met.

Minsheng appeared at my side and put a hand on my shoulder. I turned and realized the battle hadn't ended.

"You did everything you could, but I'm afraid there is more to do."

I nodded, knowing I could save more lives if I acted swiftly.

I lifted Kirdash's body and raised it high enough that

everyone could see it, then took control of the air to project my words.

"Kirdash is dead," I yelled, getting everyone's attention. "No one is forcing you to fight on. Our fight wasn't with anyone but him. He enslaved our bonded mythicals, and he enslaved many elves, gnomes, dwarves, and centaurs. Now he can't. Any of you who have fought in his name can make a choice. Keep fighting and end up like he did, or stop fighting, go back to your planet, and live your lives in peace, taking care of yourselves."

There was a pause. I held the body there for a moment, then gently lowered him to the ground. I don't know why I did it, but I placed him neatly on a bed of earth. I then carefully grew the plants and vines nearby, bringing them over his body in a living bush until he was covered in flowers, a far more beautiful and better shrine than he deserved, given what he'd done.

Everyone looked on, then gathered around us. I turned to the dragon he'd slain and the other dead we'd not been able to heal and positioned them in one group, then built a mound around them. Minds merged with mine, and the earth elves worked with me.

Some dark elves joined in, bringing their dead as well. We honored everyone who had fallen, treating them all the same way. They were the unfortunate soldiers who had died defending what they thought was the right thing or fighting the only way they knew how.

Once that was done, people moved to go through the portals, but a dark elf general came forward.

"We have long served Kirdash and let him provide us with power in return for our loyalty. While he called himself Henera and looked after those he trusted, he was difficult to serve. If you truly intend to let us go in peace, we shall gladly do so, but know that the world we come from is harsh, and many will suffer without the aid and protection he provided."

"Then I or other allies with the strength to help will come through the portal soon and help. It's time that no one suffers and all are at peace."

The general bowed, and my mythicals and I returned the gesture.

After the dark elves went, calm washed over me. I was done. After years of fighting to be left in peace, I'd defeated the evil that was the reason I existed.

I wasn't sure what ought to follow something like that or what my world would look like now, but I was at peace, and for now, that was enough.

I'm hungry, Zephyr said. *Want to get pizza?*

Unable to help it, I burst out laughing, as did Roth, Nuri, and Sen.

Pizza was exactly what I wanted.

EPILOGUE

As water gushed down the channel carved into the mountain, I found myself grinning. A week ago, we'd fought Kirdash and defeated him, and now I stood on the side of the mountain that Nerik had called home.

When I'd first traded with him, I had promised his mountain would be provided with water and that I'd make sure he didn't have to worry about not being able to grow crops there. It seemed fitting that one of the first places we helped the elves and dark elves on the homeworld was by honoring that promise.

And we had. Cherisse, Emily, Zephyr, and I had worked with the elves here to create a system, and with Earth technology and soldiers to help us install it, there was running water and a small irrigation system. It wouldn't supply a lot of people, but the small gardens here would grow more easily.

It also meant the farm would no longer need to feed as many people, and the two could trade.

Looking down the mountain, I surveyed the land beyond. A lot of it was desert-like. The dark elf hadn't cared for the planet, but Sierrathen and many of the elves in the Sanctuary who had been responsible for growing and maintaining the great elven city had agreed to see what they could do for it.

There was hope, and the dark elves were working with us to provide for everyone in the meantime.

"It won't be perfect overnight," Zephyr said, speaking aloud—a rare thing for him. "But it will get better if we help them."

"I can't wait to see it in a year. Or ten."

"It's impressive now," he replied. "You should see what they're doing at the palace I was held in. They said they've found eggs. Large ones. With scales."

"Dragon eggs?" I asked, wondering how he had kept something like that from me.

"I knew you'd be torn, wanting to keep your promise here. It won't hurt for them to wait a few more days. The dark elves want me to come and confirm one way or another as soon as I can."

I lifted an eyebrow, wondering if that was an invitation to go see them. Dragon eggs. Would some hatch?

Zephyr read my thoughts as Sen bounded onto my shoulder. Nuri and Roth took to the air.

Grinning, he leaped off the edge of the mountain, powering up with his air abilities. I eagerly followed, using the air to propel myself into the sky.

He transformed into a large bronze dragon, gliding along beneath me. I moved toward him, and the two of us came together in the air. Nuri and Roth settled into his slipstream.

The elven homeworld was still hurting, and we'd lost a lot liberating it, but there was hope.

And hope was enough.

ACKNOWLEDGMENTS

Once again, there are so many amazing people to thank for this series that I am very worried that I'll forget someone important.

This series started thanks to JN Chaney at Variant and his advise to me at a time when I really needed to hear it. Without his suggestion to take the style I had and the voice I was developing to write an urban fantasy series and to explain to me that the perfect genre did exist for me, I just hadn't noticed.

And then to LMBPN and everyone who handles my books and covers, including Michael, Kelly, Lynne, David and Robin. Without this amazing team of people, my books wouldn't be anywhere near as good or making the readers so happy and I'm so grateful.

And to David for all the series plot help. You make me feel excited about each new series I start and talking about them with you always helps me clear my head of the worries and focus in on what would make a good story. I love our plotting moments.

To Bryan and Bear for being with me while I wrote in various different ways. Sometimes the company and the conversation while I wrangle words in the right order is exactly what I need and you're both amazing at being the right sort of company.

To all my readers for reading this far. Thank you for coming on this journey. I know this is the final book in this particular story but I hope you'll continue to trust me with your emotions and time and come on another journey with me and read about some more of the characters in my head and heart.

My tiny humans who give me a reason every day to try and make this world a better place in some way. I want to leave them a better life than when I started. To give them a world I can be proud of, and that starts in lots of little ways and in my heart. I'm trying to be a better person for them and I hope that comes out in my characters too.

And to God, who helps me with everything else. I wouldn't have got through this year without Him. It's been a wild ride and not one I want to repeat. But I'm still here, I still have some hope and I still want to keep trying to make this world a better place. There's a lot to be said for those basics sometimes and they're all down to God holding me tightly and not letting go.

ABOUT THE AUTHOR

Jess is in the process of changing her name. She's been through a difficult year that leaves her wanting a fresh start and a chance to be the person she's always meant to be. Over the next little while all her books will be moving to Talia Beckett and you'll find all future releases under this author name.

Talia was born in the quaint village of Woodbridge in the UK, has spent some of her childhood in the States and now resides near the beautiful Roman city of Bath. She lives with her two tiny humans (one boy and one girl) and near an amazing group of friends who support her career and life choices.

During her still relatively short life Talia has displayed an innate curiosity for learning new things and has therefore studied many subjects, from maths and the sciences, to history and drama. Talia now works full time as a writer and mummy, incorporating many of the subjects she has an interest in within her plots and characters.

When she's not busy with work and keeping her tiny humans alive she can often be found with friends, playing with miniature characters, dice and pieces of paper covered in funny stats and notes about fictional adventures her figures have been on.

You can find out more about the author and her

upcoming projects by joining her on facebook, by watching her live D&D streams, or emailing her via books@jessmountifield.co.uk. Talia loves hearing from a happy fan so please do get in touch!

Talia is also opening up her discord for fans to come chat about what she's up to, and see a few sneak peaks of future work. There's also a chance to become one of her beta readers. If you'd like to check that out you can do so here

Connect with Jess Mountifield/Talia Beckett

Mailing list sign up
Facebook group.
Discord group
Actual play D&D stream: Twitch or Youtube
Email address: contact me here.

BOOKS BY JESS MOUNTIFIELD

Books by Jess Mountifield/Talia Beckett

Already published

Urban Fantasy

Dragon of Shadow and Air:

Air Bound

Shadow Sworn

Dragon Souled

Earth Bound

Night Sworn

Dryad Souled

Water Bound

Day Sworn

Pegasus Souled

Fire Bound

Light Sworn

Phoenix Souled

Fantasy

Tales of Ethanar:

Wandering to Belong (Tale 1)

Innocent Hearts (Tale 2 & 3)

For Such a Time as This (Tale 4)

A Fire's Sacrifice (Tale 5)

Winter Series:

The Hope of Winter (Tale 6.05)

The Fire of Winter (Tale 6.1)

Guild of the Eternal Flame:

Wayfarer's Sanctuary

Protector's Secret

Healer's Oath

Other Fantasy:

The Initiate (under Holly Lujah)

Writing with Dawn Chapman:

Jessica's Challenge (#5 in the Puatera Online series)

Dahlia's Shadow (#6 in the Puatera Online series)

Lila's Revenge (#7 in the Puatera Online series)

Star Trail:

Hunted

Sherdan series:

Sherdan's Prophecy

Sherdan's Legacy

Sherdan's Country

Sherdan's Road (A short story in the anthology 'The End of the Road')

The Slave Who'd Never Been Kissed (A short in the charity anthology 'Imaginings')

New Beginnings

Santa's Little Space Pirate

In the multi-author Adamanta series:

Episode 1 – Adamanta

Episode 3 – Excelsior

Episode 8 – Phoenix

Episode 13 – New Contacts

Episode 17 – Sacrifice

Other:

Clues, Claws and Christmas

Non-Fic:

How to Write Lots, and Get Sh*t Done: the Art of Not Being a Flake

Find purchase links here

Coming soon:

Urban Fantasy:

Dragon Apparent:

Dragon Missing

Dragon Betrayed

Sci-Fi:

Fringe Colonies:

Alliance

Haven

Rebellion

Rebirth

Reclamation

Fantasy

(Tales of Ethanar):

The Pursuit of Winter (#2 in the Winter series, Tale 6.2)

Books under Amelia Price

Mycroft Holmes Adventures:

The Hundred Year Wait

The Unexpected Coincidence

The Invisible Amateur

The Female Charm

The Reluctant Knight

The Ambitious Orphan

The Unconventional Honeymoon Gift

The Family Reunion

The Immortal Problem

The Unremarkable Assistant

Coming soon:

Mycroft 11

OTHER BOOKS FROM LMBPN PUBLISHING

Sign up for the LMBPN email list to be notified of new releases and special deals!

https://lmbpn.com/email/

For a complete list of books by LMBPN please visit:

https://lmbpn.com/books-by-lmbpn-publishing/